The Women of AngelFire

"The hap ... *is*
pouri ...

Fic
K

7/13
B&T
14.95

Song Credits

Great Balls of Fire –
Written by Otis Blackwell and Jack Hammer
Made famous by Jerry Lee Lewis

Ain't No Mountain High Enough –
Written by Nickolas Ashford and Ashlee Simpson
Made famous by Marvin Gaye and Tammi Terrell

When Will I Be Loved –
Written by the Everly Brothers
Made famous by the Everly Brothers

For my daughters
Denise, Michelle, and Heather

And to Beatrice, my mother,
who has stood by me through everything.

Acknowledgements

Ms. Cynthia Sands, *who I believe was brought to me by God*, edited this book with such care for the characters, with flawless integrity and unfailing professionalism. Her collaborative support was more than I had a right to expect.

My sincerest gratitude goes to Beatrice Grizzel, Beatrice Quesada, Cara Fisher, Denise Sahagun, Jean Curtis, Judy Woodruff, Sandra Patterson, Terry Fisher, and Wendy Marcot, who were each readers of early drafts of the manuscript. Their insightful responses led to the deepening of characters, wider perspectives, and even a few name changes. One astute comment from Wendy Marcot created an entire chapter and the movement of a peripheral character to the foreground, who then became an integral part of the series.

A grand note of gratitude from my heart goes to Reverend Rosella Turner, Suzann Owings, and Kate Alves, as women who define the art of encouragement.

Lastly, I must tenderly thank my brother Douglas Keyes, posthumously, who talked me into writing fiction in the first place, and to Linda Keyes, also posthumously, who, while in chemotherapy, read the manuscript and stated that *The Women of AngelFire* gave her a place to go each night where she could escape, to laugh and dream.

My desire for the reader is to have friends like the women listed on this page.

Introduction

You are invited to meet the Women of AngelFire – a novel series, in which the characters include a multi-ethnic, multi-cultural company of kindred spirits, who meet annually for a retreat in the pristine mountains of northern New Mexico.

Although the company of friends arrives with intentions to console their host, who is grieving over the tragic loss of her husband, each soon reveals her own crisis, placing all at turning points in their own lives. Their individual quandaries are challenged by their collective wisdom, buoyed by a sense of humor, and encouraged through transformational insights and revelations. Each is given a golden opportunity through the beneficence of love.

Originally written as a tribute to long term friendships, the series has evolved into something more. Each of the female characters represents different aspects of the feminine nature as taught by the late Ann Meyer-Makeever, D.D., who also taught me that there is a loving answer to every question.

Best-selling novelist Anne Lamott once stated in an interview that everyone she knows becomes a character in her books, yet to date, no one has ever recognized themselves. The Women of AngelFire are loosely based on some of my own long term friendships. Acceptance and respect of each other's individuality, wisdom, and choices, are the keys to the longevity of these relationships.

My hope for the reader is that you too, have heart-centered women friends with whom you can laugh, cry and sing. May your friends love and support you as my friends have done for me and as The Women of AngelFire do for each other.

The Women of AngelFire

Caroline

Candles lit
Wine poured
Lavender mists rising from the hot steeping-tub
Crimson silk slid gently from her shoulders, falling softly to the floor
She pressed "play" then stepped into the water
Deep into the water...she captured a pure moment of silence
Rising... she heard the music
It was his music, not hers...
A sip of a Santa Fe Syrah and slow exhale
Resting her head on the bath pillow, she gazed at a thousand stars
    in a half-moon sky

> *"Crazy...crazy for feeling so lonely..."*
> *"Crazy...crazy for feeling so blue ..."*

And she waited

As the music finished...she tilted her head slightly to the left and
whispered...

"Frank...Are you with me? Frank?

Carmen & Julia

*T*wo floors below, in the kitchen of the Inn at AngelFire, Carmen Robles gazed at that same half-moon sky, but her thoughts were elsewhere. Her long black hair lay with the luster of satin down the middle of her back. She made tea while her husband, JB, finished with the horses in the barn. Her thoughts were interrupted as Julia, Caroline's older sister, entered the room.

There was no mistaking that Julia and Caroline were sisters, with both having curly auburn hair and almond-shaped brown eyes. Julia was in a sage terry robe which had a merlot colored AngelFire insignia embroidered on the breast pocket. Her chicly cropped hair was wrapped in a matching towel. "Hmmm...What kind of tea is that?" Julia asked.

"Desert Grass," Carmen answered. "I don't think you want this."

"Does it have some kind of Zuni medicinal cure in it?" Julia quipped, "Because if it does, I want some."

"No, it doesn't...it is just a little bitter, that's all," Carmen answered. She took another sip and reset a flame under the tea kettle. "I'll get you something English."

"Will you sit with me for a minute?" asked Julia.

"I will until JB comes in," said Carmen. "Did you have a nice visit with Caroline?"

"I did, and as much as we tease each other, there has always been an unspoken understanding between us. I guess I'll always try to watch over her, no matter how old we are. That is, until I'm too old, have lost my senses and she has to watch over me!

There's that music again. Is your husband in the barn dancing with the ghost of Patsy Cline?" asked Julia.

"No," Carmen laughed, "But he's probably talking to the spirit of Frank Amoroso. The music is coming from upstairs. It's Caroline...she plays it nearly every night when she bathes. Frank loved Patsy Cline. She's still having a hard time, Julia. Next week it will be a year."

"What is she doing up there with that music?" Julia asked.

"Probably having a good cry or maybe discussing the future of the Inn with Frank," Carmen answered. "Sometimes I feel like he's still here...still running this place."

"I'll talk to her in the morning. She needs to get away from here for a few weeks," replied Julia.

"Some of her friends will be here this week," said Carmen. "She's hosting her annual retreat for them. Maybe when they leave, she'll be ready to go with you."

"Really, who's coming? Anyone I know?" Julia asked.

"Just talk to her in the morning. JB is coming in from the barn, and we're going to a Council meeting tonight. Problems with the high school, I think. Will we see you tomorrow?" asked Carmen.

"I'll be here until about ten tomorrow morning, and then we're driving to the Albuquerque airport."

"Good, we'll see you at breakfast.

Julia, I think Caroline is going to have to make some decisions about the Inn. JB and I would have loved to have seen this place bustling with families this summer. She held up very well and was great with the people that were already booked, but we are running with about half the number of guests as last year. I don't know how long she can afford this. I don't know how long she and my husband want to mourn the loss of Frank, either. They're both still in a lot of pain and neither one of them will talk about it." her voice broke off quickly as she heard the latch on the back door.

JB, a tall, muscular Zuni Native American, whose rugged face said he had been through more than one would want to know, entered the room. "I'll wash up and we'll leave in a few minutes," he said to Carmen.

"Julia, how was your ride today?"

"Well, it was beautiful *and* everything I expected, having had my butt slapped by leather for an hour. I have never, ever, been able to ride a horse smoothly. I think Caroline enjoyed watching me suffer, too."

JB turned away to hide a grin, and then asked, "Is there anything you need before we go?"

"Nothing, JB...Thanks. You two go on and have a nice evening. I'm going to bed early. Thanks for the update Carmen. She puts up a great front. I guess I didn't realize...I promise I'll talk to Caroline in the morning."

At eight-thirty the next morning, Julia found Caroline in the barn...that beautiful, immaculate barn. There certainly was nothing rustic about it. Frank had it designed with the same architecture as the Inn. It housed eight stalls, with four for their golden palomino horses and one for the chestnut foal, still rooming in with its mother. Another stall stored mountain bikes, and yet another had snowboards, skis, and golf clubs - something for every guest. A locked storage room held seasonal equipment and another had feed, tack and supplies. JB and the staff groomed the horses daily, maintained the barn, and performed the numerous other tasks required for the upkeep of the AngelFire Inn.

The Inn was unlike anything in the area. The entire property resembled an old world country estate similar to those found in the French Alps near the Italian border. The three story inn was both stylish and comfortable, and welcomed guests all year round. When first opened, it was operated as a bed and breakfast. Within a year, Frank realized that they would need to expand to achieve the Inn's full potential. By the third year, they added five private bungalows and three additional buildings that functioned as small versions of a music and theater hall, craft and game zone, and last but not least, the spa, complete with a hot tub and sauna. They were soon running at full capacity with a rotation of thirty to forty guests at a time, which often called for impromptu gatherings for music, heaps of nature scrapbooking and family board games. Weary skiers and snowboarders nearly always headed straight for the spa.

The pines that lined the long circular entrance drive hid the grandeur of the rural chateau at AngelFire from the main highway. Frank and Caroline preferred an understated elegance and chose not to compete with nature's show of splendor. The stately exteriors were neutral in tone and featured stone masonry that exuded old world craftsmanship. The only additional color on the exterior was the carnelian red on all the doors and shutters, and this color was repeated on all the trim of the buildings on the grounds. Behind the Inn was a hillside with a thick stand of Aspens which glistened in the golden autumn and gloriously crowned the chimney-dotted roofline.

The interiors were a splendid blend of textures, with oversized stone fireplaces, wood and stone floors, brick accents, and leather upholstery pieces. A variety of Native American rugs were often the only patterns in a room. The art was a collection of Native American crafts, and original scenic landscape paintings found in the art galleries of Santa Fe and Taos. Comfort was the character of the AngelFire Inn. Caroline made only small seasonal changes in the main dining room and bungalows, but thoroughly *decked the halls* for the Christmas holidays.

My sister lives in a dream world, literally and figuratively, thought Julia as she approached Caroline in the barn. She looked at Caroline for a moment before she spoke and thought she seemed thinner than at their last visit, even a little frail, but decided not to say anything about it. Caroline barely noticed Julia's presence.

"Don't get any ideas about another saddle-spanking for me today," said Julia as she moved toward her sister. "Once a year is enough. How about a walk instead?"

"Sure, we could hike up to the lake," Caroline answered, feigning a smile. She led the way from the barn to the well-marked path toward the lake. The crisp morning air was an invigorating reminder of the qualities of living in these pristine mountains.

As Caroline and Julia walked, they embraced the beauty of the aspens and pines and inhaled the fresh fragrance of wildflowers. Delicate scents of buttercups, asters and rare wild lilies filled the air all the way to lake. Through nature the sisters found a peaceful common ground. They walked quietly, without words to distract them from the beauty before them. When they arrived at the lake, Julia spread her shawl on the ground and invited her sister to sit for a few moments.

"This is so serene and picturesque...it is absolutely heavenly here in the summer. I understand why you continue to stay."

"Where else would I want to be?" Caroline asked.

"I don't know...maybe a place where you could start a new life? It must be hard for you to run the Inn without Frank," Julia answered softly and compassionately. Her heart ached for her sister, who seemed much too young to be a widow.

"Carmen and JB have been my saving grace, and I couldn't or wouldn't do this without them. They are as much a part of this place as I am. Remember, Frank and JB were building the Inn before I married Frank. Carmen and I came on board about the same time. The four of us built this business together, and we're like a family, you know. They have been a real comfort this last year. Frank's death has been hard on each of us." Caroline paused...took a deep breath, and continued, "I *like* my life at AngelFire, *and* I'm not ready to make any changes."

"I understand honey – it must be both hard to leave *and* hard to stay. Do you think you'd like to take a little vacation? David and I have tickets for a cruise to Alaska, and I made a reservation for you. I'd really like you to consider coming with us. It would be a complete change of scenery, and I think it would be good for you. And it's on us...you don't have to worry about paying for a thing," she offered.

"Julia, I can pay my own way. Frank left me plenty of money. I'm fine, really."

"Are you sure? If your business isn't running at full occupancy, how can you be making a profit?"

"When Frank died, Robbie told me he would take care of everything and to take as much time as I needed to adjust. Eventually, I'll go in to see him and we'll make some decisions." Caroline answered.

"Are you saying that you don't know exactly what you have to work with?" Julia asked.

"Julia, I'm sure it's fine. Robbie pays all the bills. He called me to set up a meeting and also said that I have nothing to worry about. I will go and see where I stand...I promise." Caroline gave Julia a hug and said, "Please don't worry about me."

"Caroline, it's almost a year. You are a young widow who has lost a husband you've deeply loved. You don't know exactly what your finances are, and you're running a business at half its potential. You live alone up there in that apartment when Carmen and JB go home and...and you're fine? Don't you get lonely up there at night?"

"Well, to tell you the truth. I really don't feel like I am alone. I think Frank is still here with me. I know you might think I'm crazy, but I feel like he's actually helping me manage the Inn – and that he always will," Caroline answered.

"Okay – that's it." Julia squared off with Caroline and took her by the shoulders. "Look, I saw '*The Ghost and Mrs. Muir*' seven times, too. You, like Mrs. Muir, are still a young and beautiful woman. I will not let you waste the next thirty years waiting to walk off into the clouds with Frank Amoroso. Honey, Frank's life ended tragically – but it has ended. There are many things you could still do with your life. You had a great career before Frank. AngelFire was Frank's dream. You can...*not...keep this Gull Cottage for him.*"

Eyes brimming with tears, Caroline cleared her throat and answered her sister, "I know you think I'm crazy. I shouldn't have told you that Frank is still here. You haven't forgotten when Grandpa Freddie died – right? Remember, we both thought he was still in the house."

"He did that so Grandma Tootsie couldn't sell the house and run off with his brother, Uncle Ben. Honestly, I think it was Uncle Ben who burned the place down. You know they ran away together anyway, no matter how they tried to hide it from us kids. God, she was eighty!" said Julia. She smiled at the thought of it. Julia was always the understanding and protective sister. She decided she would now keep a closer eye on Caroline to see how this played out.

"Okay, I know that you're right about some things. I promise I will make an appointment with Robbie and find out what my financial situation is, and then I'll think about what I need to do. One thing at a time, okay Julia? I have no idea what else I would do with my life. Frank and I *love* AngelFire."

"Frank *loved* – you *love*. Just make sure your finances are okay so that you can keep the Inn if you want to. You've had the Inn for only twelve years. You must still have a huge balance on that mortgage."

"Well, Frank took care of the finances, so I don't really know. Ugh – and I just gave you a reason for ten more minutes of this conversation, didn't I? Can we just stop now?" Caroline pleaded.

"All right, let's get back to the Inn and I'll get my luggage," Julia conceded, as she looked at her watch.

"*Thank you, God,*" Caroline whispered.

The return hike to AngelFire was as silent and calm as the ascent. Julia spotted a doe prodding a fawn toward a higher trail, and turned to look at Caroline. Caroline had already noticed the deer and whispered to her sister, "I get it and I love you for it, too."

Upon their return, Carmen had a fruit salad waiting for them, and JB had the AngelFire guest van cleaned and waiting in the driveway. He'd already loaded Julia's luggage. When all good-byes were said and hugs given, they were off to the Albuquerque airport.

"We didn't really need this big guest van for this trip, did we? You can't be getting much mileage on this," said Julia.

"Actually, I'm picking up some guests for this week. We're completely booked."

"Uh – are these paying guests?" asked Julia. "Don't lie. I already know you're hosting your annual retreat with your friends. So who's coming this year?"

"Marti is coming." Caroline answered. "I haven't seen her since the ...."

"Marti – that's wonderful!" Julia interrupted. "Is she still waiting for the love of her life?"

Caroline frowned. "Who isn't, Julia? Marti's spent her whole life devoted to her son, Erik, and to her music. Now that Erik's added grandchildren to her life, she's even busier. She seems quite content with things just as they are."

"Is there anyone else coming in this week who I might know?"

"Siggy is driving in from Colorado tomorrow," Caroline added.

"Don't you think that woman is sort of whacky? Did she send you that disgusting pineapple popcorn at Christmas? It was absolutely soggy."

"We all got some. You're right; it was pretty bad, but hey – she's been trying to win another contest. Leave her alone. That woman's heart of gold has to help her win something eventually," responded Caroline.

"She has been trying to win those contests for nearly ten years. She is persistent. We'll have to give her that."

"It could happen for her. Sooner or later she will come up with something great. She has to; her dreams are all she has left...at least she still has dreams – right?" said Caroline.

"Yes...so who else is coming? Will I see them at the airport?"

"Kate should be arriving with Marti, and Diana is flying in to Santa Fe tomorrow. Nicole might be here by the weekend."

"Diana! Of all your friends, she's probably the only normal one in the lot!" Julia teased.

"There is nothing normal about the life of a woman married to a famous televangelist," said Caroline. "*Please*...she has always had the role of being the minister's graceful wife. That's not always normal. I don't think I have ever seen her angry or heard her say a harsh word. How normal is that?"

"Well, what about Dr. Kate? Is she still running that holistic healing center?" Julia asked. "May I remind you that she gave me some kind of herbal concoction last year during the funeral? It was supposed to calm my nerves. Instead, I slept through the entire reception."

And that is how she became my very best friend, Caroline whispered under her breath. "Kate gave me some of that concoction too, and it really does work; but then you already know that. Her clinic in Sonoma has become a renowned healing center and is incredibly successful. She sounded exhausted when I last spoke to her, so I'm glad she'll be coming out for a rest."

"Is Nicole still teaching math or science in Chicago?" Julia asked. "Since she wasn't able to make it to the funeral, I haven't heard you say much about her this year."

"She said she has a big announcement, so I think she'll try her best to come out by Thursday," Caroline answered.

"She's probably '*coming out*' all right," Julia mumbled.

"I heard that and if you don't watch it, I'll put some herbal concoction of my own in that water bottle, and they will have to carry you off that plane," teased Caroline.

"Have you heard from anyone in Frank's family?" Julia asked.

"Well, not in a while. His brothers, Giovanni and Sal, each called a few weeks after the funeral to see if I needed anything."

"Be careful of those Mafia boys, Caroline. They can be very charming," Julia warned.

"For the very last time, Julia, Frank was not part of a Mafia family. Have you and David been watching the Sopranos again? Honestly, where do you get these things?"

"Well, they are an Italian family that moved from New York to Las Vegas in the early '50s. Frank never took you on his trips to Vegas. You know very little about his life before you met him, and a limousine with five men in black suits and dark glasses came to the funeral. Did they stay for the dinner? I wouldn't know because one of your friends sedated me and I missed it. How do you know that Frank wasn't sequestered in AngelFire as part of the Witness Protection Program?"

Caroline whispered "Be quiet Julia, he can hear you."

Julia blanched, then gasped, "WHAT? Is he in the car – right now?...Stop the car! I mean it Caroline. STOP THE CAR!"

Caroline pulled over to the right edge of the road, trying as best she could to hold back her laughter.

Julia got out of the car and slid open the van door to the back-seat. "Go into the Light, Frank," she shouted. *"Into the Light!* It is best for you and for Caroline. Don't do this Frank."

Caroline could no longer hold in her laughter, as she saw that her sister was once again trying to protect her. She got out of the car, walked over to Julia and put an arm around her shoulder then said, "He's not here Julia. I'm sorry, I shouldn't have done that. You know how I get when you talk about Frank's family. I don't care who they are or who they were. They never interfered with our lives and yes, he did not take me to visit them, and no he was *not* in the Witness Protection Program – Okay? He's not here in the car, either. Come on, let's get to the airport."

The sisters regained their composure and returned to the car. Caroline looked over her shoulder and hesitated slightly. She started the van and headed out on the highway toward the Albuquerque airport, keeping an eye on the image in the rear view mirror.

About thirty feet away, stood a specter of light in the outline of a man. It remained still, barely noticeable...as...*it watched them.*

Marti

"Alone, all alone
Nobody, but nobody
Can make it out here alone."

- Maya Angelou

*T*he uniqueness of the Albuquerque airport is unexpected and a portal to the culture of the Southwest. Works of indigenous art reflecting the distinctive character of the region are displayed throughout. Numerous gift shops and eateries reveal the unique culture and styles of New Mexico. The airport's main corridor hosts a steep set of escalators that ascend for departing passengers and descend for arriving passengers. Marti Westerlund and Kate O'Neil were about to make their descent, just as Julia was arriving at the top of the ascending staircase.

Julia saw them first and called out, "Marti! – Kate!"

Marti responded with a warmhearted smile and waved. "Wave to Julia...she's on your left," she whispered to Kate.

"What? Did I miss something?" responded Kate. "I can hardly keep my eyes open. Can you see Caroline yet?" Kate wore over-sized sunglasses to cover the dark shadows of exhaustion that lay under her eyes. A tie-dyed scarf covered her red, curly slept-on hair, as she had taken an early morning flight from San Francisco to Los Angeles in order to join Marti on the flight to Albuquerque.

Marti was the first to find Caroline. She was near the foot of the escalators admiring an encased display of Zuni pottery on loan from a Santa Fe art museum. After jubilant hellos, hugs, and baggage retrieval, the trio set out for the long trip to AngelFire with plans to stop for lunch in Santa Fe.

Kate opted for the back seat of the AngelFire van, where she could stretch out her weary body. "Sorry girls, I have hardly slept for three days in preparation for this week off. My health and well-ness clinic just may be the death of me. If you don't mind, I'd like to sleep a little on the way to Santa Fe." She laid her head on the flaxseed pillow she'd carried with her all the way from Sonoma. Within seconds, her jaw slacked and a soft snore signaled her descent into oblivion.

Marti turned from the front passenger seat to check on Kate. "Do you think we should strap her in so she doesn't fall on the floor and impale herself on something?"

"Let's just make sure there is nothing back there that can hurt her," Caroline answered.

After securing Kate, Marti returned to her seat and admitted, "I think I am almost as tired as she is. Erik and Laney had another baby girl last night. I was at the hospital until two o'clock this morning."

"Congratulations! Two granddaughters - how wonderful! She wasn't due for two more weeks – right? Is everybody happy and healthy?" asked Caroline.

"Yes, and she is beautiful and black like her Grandma Martha."

"And you're safe again," added Caroline. "What would you have done if she came out blonde and blue-eyed like her Grandpa Erik?"

"She didn't, and I didn't realize it was time for our annual conversation about Erik senior. I thought we usually did that in November," answered Marti.

Taking the focus off herself, she turned to Caroline. "What about you? You've been sounding good lately; but honey, I didn't realize you had lost so much weight. You are looking *widow-thin*," said Marti.

"Well, I was just about to tell you how great you look. Your braids are gorgeous, and longer than usual, *and* it sounds like you have you been talking to Julia," Caroline responded. "I'm fine. I just weighed too much before. How is the music composition coming along? Any word yet?"

"It's too soon to know just yet. I don't expect to hear anything before mid-September," said Marti. "I think it is my best work so far. I really felt something powerful in this piece. The professor thinks I have a very good chance. Can you believe that? Me, Martha-Naomi-*who?* - Westerlund, performing an original composition with the Pacific Symphony; I hope he is right this time!"

"Marti, I'm so proud of you for what you have accomplished. Just creating something that qualified for this competition is fantastic. I know how hard you've worked for this, and I'm sure it is a brilliant masterpiece. And when they ask you to play it on stage, I'll fly out there and be your best audience. I'll bet Julia and Katie will be there, too. All of us, your family, will be right there with you," said Caroline.

"Thank you Caroline, let's just let it be for now. Please don't say anything to the others yet. While we're keeping things quiet, and while Kate is still sleeping, who else knows about your little visits from Frank?" Marti asked.

"I made the mistake of telling Julia this morning," said Caroline. "It wasn't such a good idea. This isn't easy, but I know when he is present. I feel him with me and sometimes I even see him. I don't know how this works, or how long it will last or if it is even right. I just know that I feel his love, and it's like he's returned to me.

"Do you think he is trying to tell you something?" Marti asked.
"Maybe...," she answered.

⚜

Caroline met Martha Westerlund while at a summer job as an office temp at a CPA firm in Bloomfield Hills, Michigan. It was the early 70's and a stimulating time of political and human rights activism. Born Martha Naomi Westerlund, the daughter of a prominent Baptist minister, was home for the summer from Howard University, where she was studying to become an educator. Something of a musical prodigy, Martha had become the church organist for her father's ministry at the age of thirteen. Unfortunately, it was the only kind of music he allowed her to practice, which precluded her from qualifying for any one of the renowned schools of music. Martha, the dutiful daughter, had accepted that her destiny would most likely always include being her father's church organist.

Caroline, who lived at home, attended school at the Cranbrook Institute as a natural history major. Her uncle, who was a partner at the accounting firm, gave her a summer job each year, hoping she would change her major from nature's science to economics. He had proudly hinted that new changes in policies for women might pave the way for a great career with his firm. Both young women dated interns and junior accountants and frequently dragged themselves to work after only a few hours of sleep. They would often meet in the ladies restroom and tease each other about their escapades.

Then, for Martha, the unexpected happened. Erik Olsen, a handsome Swedish foreign exchange student, fell in love with her. They dated exclusively for two months, and he nicknamed her Marti. Then, she too, fell..."Truly, madly, deeply," she confided in Caroline. Erik's student visa would expire in September, and he wanted to take Marti back to Sweden with him for "*marriage, kids, and the whole package!*" During their third month together, Marti had to muster the courage to face her parents and tell them that she'd fallen in love and was going to give up her education to follow a blond-haired, blue-eyed boy, and live four thousand miles away from them.

The expected drama ensued, with a continuous flood of tears from her mother and the unrelenting fury of her father. The wrath of the great Reverend Westerlund was not to be taken lightly, and letting Erik present his case was forbidden. Marti was not shocked or even surprised, but Erik was distraught and vowed to somehow steal her away. He took her to City Hall to apply for a passport and visa. They would marry in Stockholm, Sweden. Marti withdrew from her family and ruminated on what was best for her and for Erik. He had another two years of school ahead of him and so did she. Her mother pleaded with her to wait until after graduation from college to marry. It was the only rational thing either of her parents had said to her since the announcement.

Then, to complicate matters further, Marti discovered that she was pregnant. Frozen with fear, she knew her parents would be horrified. Once daddy's little angel, but now defiled, she would disgrace the family. What would the congregation think? With her head spinning, her heart wounded, and her stomach churning...she chose not to tell Erik. Her future may be ruined, she thought, but she would not ruin his.

Caroline walked into the ladies restroom at the office one morning and heard vomiting coming from one of the stalls. Marti finally emerged, tears running down her cheeks. Within seconds Caroline intuited the pregnancy and the enormity of this crisis for her friend. She persuaded Marti to meet with her after work for dinner and promised her that she would help. Caroline decided to use the afternoon to explore some options for Marti. She made a few telephone calls and prepared herself to be the reasonable half of their conversation. However, it did not go as well as she had planned.

"No, we cannot talk to my parents together. No, we will not tell Erik, yet. No, no abortion."

Caroline made one last offer. "I am going to California to visit my sister Julia before I go back to college. Why don't you come with me, and we'll sort this out in a fresh environment. Julia is always my best sounding board. She's ten years older, worldlier, much wiser than us, and I trust her."

After three days of pleading with her mother and father, assuring them that Erik was returning to Sweden, and that she would return to college, her parents finally agreed to Caroline's plan. So, on a hot and muggy morning in late August 1974, Caroline and Marti set out for California by train. The night before they left, Marti, heartbroken and promising to write, said goodbye to Erik. She said goodbye to her parents at the train station in Detroit. It was the last time she ever saw them, and on March 18, 1975, Erik Jr. was born in Los Angeles.

Caroline transferred to UCLA, switched her major to sociology. Marti got a job as a church organist and enrolled at the Los Angeles Academy of Music and the two young women embarked upon a new life together in California. Both sets of parents were devastated. Julia turned out to be their greatest support and helped them with housing and employment. She also spoke to the parents, declaring that within a year both girls would be too homesick to stay in California. Julia also kept Marti's secret. It was the early 1970's, and children born without fathers were considered illegitimate. Both the mothers and their children were often shunned, treated poorly, and considered unacceptable by mainstream society. So, when Erik was old enough to ask about his father, Marti told him that his father had been a soldier, who had died in the Vietnam War. Julia and Caroline reluctantly agreed to support her story.

As the years went by, Marti quietly, privately repressed her feelings for Erik's father and never tried to contact him.

⚜

It was out of a conversation with Marti that the idea for the annual AngelFire retreats began. Since Caroline and Frank had married on a trip to Italy, Caroline was excited to have her friends meet Frank, see AngelFire Inn and witness the new life they had created together. She invited Marti first, and her response had been, "I'd like to bring Siggy. She could use a vacation and would love to see you. Actually, why don't you just let me know when Kate is coming and we'll just come then." Caroline was inspired and added Diana and Nicole to the list. Thus, the first annual friends retreat at AngelFire Inn was created.

❧

"Are you hungry?" Caroline asked as they turned off the highway toward Santa Fe. "I have to pick up a few things, and I thought we'd try a new restaurant. Why don't you take a tissue back there and wipe the drool off of Kate's face before we wake her up."

As Marti began the task of making her friend presentable, she laughingly said "Nurse Marti assisting Dr. Woo-Woo; coming right up...Dr. Woo-Woo, paging Dr. Woo-Woo...Code Green...food...wake up please."

Kate

"Friends are the family you choose for yourself."

Edna Buchanan

Kate ignored Marti's teasing and pulled herself together. Readjusting her scarf and sunglasses, she appeared as if deliberately traveling incognito. "I think I could sleep for the next three days. Did I miss anything important? Switch seats with me Marti, okay?"

"We're stopping for lunch in Santa Fe," Caroline said, while Kate moved to the front passenger seat.

"Marti has another grandbaby! Isn't that wonderful?" said Kate.

"Don't start..." Marti advised, as she took a center seat.

"I'm just jealous," Kate answered. "No husband, no kids, no grandkids...and I'm not even a nun! Isn't that the antithesis of my parochial education?

"Katie, you have a degree, a clinic, more patients than you can handle, and you're doing what you love," Caroline reminded her.

"And it seems I've been doing it forever...I honestly don't remember much of what came before this part of my life. I never thought that once I got to my fifties I would still be working this hard. I teach healthy living – right? Ugh - I promise I'll stop complaining and just enjoy this week. Everyone needs a change of scenery now and then." Kate yawned, again.

As they entered the shaded courtyard encircled by art galleries and specialty shops, they breathed in the Santa Fe culture. Just as they were being seated for lunch, a voice called out to Caroline.

"Caroline?" he called. "Caroline Amoroso!"

Caroline turned her head to see a short raven-haired man, dressed in jeans, a cashmere sweater, western boots, and Armani sunglasses, heading her way. It was Robbie Collicci. *Oh God, she thought.* She smiled and waved as he was quickly approaching. "Hello Robbie, what a surprise. It's nice to see you. May I introduce you to my friends? Marti, Kate – Robbie Collicci. Robbie manages the finances for AngelFire."

Kate immediately put her hand out to greet him. "How do you do," she said in a sultry voice, which turned the heads of both Caroline and Marti.

Robbie took off his glasses revealing his dark brown eyes, which were now glued to the mystery woman, while he acknowledged Marti. Then he returned to Caroline and said, "Can you come to my office this week?" he asked. "It's not anything urgent and it's all good, but it *is* important. You have some decisions to make."

Before Caroline could respond, Kate said, "I'll take you Caroline. I have some decisions to make too. Perhaps Mr. Collicci will help me make some decisions, too."

"I'd *love* to help you make some decisions," he stated.

"I'd love to *have you help me* make some decisions," responded Kate liltingly.

"Is it something in the air?" Marti whispered to Caroline, who was rolling her eyes.

"Well, now that we've all decided," began Caroline, "I promise I'll come to see you next week," she added, as she glared at Marti who was holding her hand over her mouth.

Robbie smiled; actually, he was beaming as he bid farewell to the women.

"Okay, who are you and what have you done with my friend Kate?" Marti asked. "Take off the scarf and glasses and reveal yourself."

Kate answered, "I have no idea what just came over me. Who *is* that darling man?"

"*Darling man?* That's our accountant. I guess I have put him off long enough. I'll make an appointment for both of us, if you promise to behave yourself," said Caroline.

"No promises. I don't know why I was so instantly attracted to him. This *never* happens to me."

"Oh, I get it," Marti said. "She wants to have vacation sex!"

"STOP IT...I don't even know what that means,." Kate answered.

"Right...Okay, let's order." Marti answered.

After a light salad luncheon and a tour of the perimeter shops and galleries, the three friends boarded the van and proceeded to the AngelFire Inn. Kate slept all the way.

❦

Caroline and Marti met Kate at UCLA in 1974, while attending a women's basketball game. It was the first year for women's basketball scholarships, and they wanted to support their team, regardless of the fact that neither of them knew anything about basketball. The bleachers were filled, mainly with female students. One of them, Kate O'Neil, noticed Marti, who by this time was "showing" and was not wearing a wedding ring. Kate introduced herself to Marti and handed her a card for a free women's clinic. Kate was a nurse, and was also volunteering at the clinic. Caroline and Marti had heard of the clinic, but were a little fearful of going there. Women's free clinics were showing up in major cities all over the country, but some had questionable reputations. Since the price was right, they agreed to check it out. Caroline just wanted birth control pills, and Marti wanted birthing options. They called Kate and she agreed to meet them for a tour. Kate spent a great deal of time with them, giving them the tour of the clinic, and discussing its mission and purpose, which was to educate women about their bodies and their choices. The days of just following whatever the usual male doctor told a woman were no longer acceptable. Woman needed more education and a greater understanding of their options. Kate assured Marti that she could receive compassionate prenatal care. Her sincerity, warmth and consideration for someone she had only met once before deeply touched both women, and their friendship grew from that first meeting at the clinic.

Marti had her baby at a traditional hospital, thanks to Julia's generosity. Kate attended the birth and sat with Caroline and Julia in the waiting room. So Erik gained an Aunt Katie, along with Aunt Caroline and Aunt Julia. Five years later, Kate left traditional medicine to study Holistic Medicine at San Francisco State University, one of the first universities on the west coast to offer the program. In the course of her training she traveled to China, Europe and South America with other seekers on a quest for natural health remedies.

In 1990, Kate opened her own practice as a naturopath, and founded a wellness center. She wisely brought in complimentary therapies, and eventually partnered with an acupuncturist, a chiropractor, massage therapists, Reiki workers, and herbalists. Always open to new pathways to health, she dedicated her life to those who came to her for help. It was her passion and believed it was her God given, life's purpose. Through experience and her deeply spiritual nature, Kate developed another aspect of her abilities and as a result was gaining quite a reputation as a medical intuitive, yet she preferred to keep this concealed. Friends like Marti, had already begun to refer to her as *Dr. Woo-Woo!*

She kept in touch with Marti, more often than the others, because she took her role of Erik's Aunt Kate seriously. Her responsibilities at the clinic left little time for catching up with friends, which was why these annual retreats were so important to her. Somehow, some way, she managed never to miss one.

❧

The women arrived at AngelFire Inn in the middle of the afternoon, and Carmen and JB were graciously waiting to welcome them. Carmen checked them in, giving Marti and Kate keys to two of the Inn's five bungalows. None of Caroline's guests were scheduled to stay in the any of the Inn's ten guest rooms. Caroline preferred to give them the added luxury and privacy of the bungalows. She advised both Kate and Marti to rest for a while, before wine at seven and dinner at eight.

Kate welcomed the additional time for further rest, and Marti mentioned that she would like to take a walk and stretch her legs after a day of sitting in airplanes followed by the long cartrip. JB escorted them, luggage in tow, along the path toward their accommodations. Carmen had provided each of the bungalows with fresh flowers, fruit, and New Mexico wines.

As they reached Bungalow #3, Kate gave Marti a quick hug and whispered, "Frank's here."

"I know," replied Marti.

Siggy

"Friends are God's way of apologizing to us for our families."

Anonymous

K ate rifled through her bags just long enough to find a nightgown. She called Carmen and asked for a wake-up call in time to dress for dinner, and then collapsed on top of the bed and immediately fell into a deep sleep.

Marti unpacked and was on her way back to the Inn when in a cloud of dust, a bright red SUV sped up the long entry drive. Carmen and Caroline came out to see who would drive so furiously. As the dust dissipated, Caroline also noticed the approach of a Mercedes stretch limousine about twenty yards behind them. Marti and Caroline gave each other a curious glance.

The SUV came to a halt, and a pair of long legs in short shorts and sandals jumped out and immediately went to the rear of the car. "I think that's Sherry, Siggy's girl," Marti said. "I'll take care of this. You go see who's in the limo."

Turning her attention to the present commotion, Marti teasingly said, "Hey girl, you get your designer butt over here and give your Aunt Marti a hug. Now just what is going on here? Are you in training for NASCAR or something?"

"Sorry Aunt Marti. I'm just trying to get this over with," answered Sherry McGann, Siggy's only daughter.

"What is that supposed to mean?" Marti asked authoritatively.

"I'll let my mother tell you all about it," she answered sarcastically.

Marti noticed that Siggy remained in the car with her head down. While JB helped Sherry with an inordinate amount of luggage and several boxes, Marti went to the passenger side of the car. "Siggy? Are you all right?" she asked.

Siggy gave no reply. As Marti opened the door, she saw her friend's eyes brimming with tears. "Oh, come on out of there... what is going on here?"

Siggy blew her nose, and then stepped out of the vehicle. Marti gave her a long hug and took her around to the front of the car. "I'm okay really, sorry to be blubbering like this," whimpered Siggy. What was left of her makeup was streaking down her face. "Is everyone here?"

"No, not yet, Kate is here and is taking a nap. Caroline and Carmen are over there talking to someone in the limo. It's just us. Diana and Nicole will be here in a day or two. Let's just get you situated, and we'll have a nice glass of wine or something. But first, I am going to speak to your daughter."

Sherry and JB were returning from Bungalow #4 where they had deposited Siggy's belongings. When they arrived at the car, Marti said, "Okay, whatever happened today, let's get over it, so you can leave each other nicely. Sherry, kindly give your mother a hug goodbye."

"Stay out of this Aunt Marti. This is not the time," Sherry responded firmly, got in the car and drove off as fast as she drove in.

"What a butthead!" Marti remarked as JB laughed out loud. Trying to lighten the situation, Marti responded to his laughter and said "Say JB, how come you never introduced me to one of your brothers? I want one like you - who'll laugh at my jokes - only without the ponytail." JB laughed again and walked away. "I mean that," she shouted.

"No you don't," he answered, without even turning around.

"So Siggy, what the heck happened to make Sherry so angry?" Marti asked.

"I don't want to talk about it," she answered. "Let's find my stuff. I have made some fake fudge for everyone. I think this one may win the big bucks."

Please God don't let it be asparagus fudge, or something equally as weird, Marti thought.

⚜

Siggy and Marti had known each other since 1975. They met at the church where Marti had found a job playing the organ. Marti played both the organ and the sympathetic roll of an army wife, waiting for her soldier husband, who was missing in action, in Vietnam. Siggy was the director of the Sunday school. She was ten years older than Marti and had two sons. Her birth name was Sigrid, and she always thought her name was too sophisticated for a plump Midwestern girl, who never quite measured up to her parent's expectations – or her own. She had followed her husband, Jonathon, to California when he had received a promotion with IBM. No one ever heard her introduce herself as Sigrid Kerrington. So "Siggy" it was, and it was a fit. She had the patience of a saint and was obsessed with crafting. The Sunday School children went home each week with elaborate creations that Siggy most likely paid for out of her own pocket. She was respected for her work and enjoyed for her bubbly personality.

While pregnant with her third child, her husband Jon disappeared with his secretary Lana, who was fifteen years younger than Jon. He and Lana had relocated to Orlando, Florida, and started a new life of their own. Siggy was devastated. Marti stood by her and attended the birth of Sherry, Siggy's only daughter. By then, Erik was a precocious toddler.

The divorce resulted in Siggy keeping the house, mortgage free, yet with her skill sets pretty much limited to crafts for children and homemaking, she was soon desperate for a job and money. Child support was hard to collect from an out of state father, especially one who showed no interest in his children and the church stipend did not go far for a single mother with three children. At one point she thought she might have to sell the house. She took a hard look at her house and all the children's toys and games she had accumulated and decided instead to open a home day care center for babies and toddlers. Church friends responded quickly, as there were not many day care centers available in the 1970's. Siggy was a natural born "mommy". She played Beatles music and kept the children dancing and playing games until they asked for their naps. Each week every child went home with a new artistic masterpiece to be displayed proudly in their home. They played organized games in her yard, and she never let any child out of her sight.

Siggy also sold Avon cosmetics, and later Mary Kay products and Tupperware, and all together, it kept the lights on. With no unforeseen disasters and with her indubitable faith, she was able to create a stable life for her family.

Marti employed her services and left Erik with Siggy until he started kindergarten. She still credits Siggy with inspiring Erik's amazing creativity. So Aunt Siggy, Aunt Marti and eventually Aunt Caroline and her sons, became each other's extended family.

In the 1980's, Siggy began entering all sorts of contests and always had a lottery ticket in her purse. Laws were changing and she didn't want a career in daycare forever. At the very least, she wanted to win a recipe contest. She tried bake-offs, chili cook-offs, and even salsa contests. She figured she would win by creating something no one had ever thought of before. A snack or candy, something fun to eat! And so it began – her friends were her taste testers; although, some considered themselves her guinea pigs.

Each Christmas the packaging of her latest creation was more elaborate than the previous year and usually more appetizing than the food stuffed inside. Her friends had to love her for staying innovative, optimistic, and sometimes even outrageous.

Siggy was the best of the group for keeping in touch with everyone. She stuck to the old fashioned art of handmade note cards, with cover art often made by children. These cards were regularly found in the mailboxes of each of her circle of friends, and, no matter what was going on in her life, the world stopped for a week, so that she could attend their annual retreat. She was a welcome presence because she never failed to bring some new project, as well as a new round of taste testing.

This year's annual retreat would bring the greatest surprises of all!

Diana

While Marti was consoling Siggy, Caroline was moving her friend Diana out of the limo, creating as little attention as possible. JB and the limousine driver hurriedly carried Diana's luggage into the Inn, while Caroline took her up to her third floor private quarters. Tears streamed from under Diana's Christian Dior sunglasses, as she moved gracefully, quietly, up the staircase.

Caroline poured a glass of wine for her friend and herself, then said "Okay honey, let's go over this again. I can't believe what I am hearing. Maybe you have misinterpreted something. Now tell me exactly what happened?"

"I'd spent the morning preparing a report for our next board meeting, and was looking for Jackson so that we could go over the financial statements. I couldn't find him, so I called his assistant Georgia, who told me to look in the choir rehearsal room. I walked over there, but I didn't see him. Then I heard some noise coming from the choir robe chamber. I opened the door and there they were – *Jackson and the new organist, Miss Elaina.* They didn't see me, but I certainly saw them."

Diana took a moment to compose herself, and then continued. "I was so startled I dropped the papers and ran out of there. I...I just ran. I know he figured out that I saw them because he's called my cell phone every half hour since. I took the bags I had already packed for this retreat and just got on a plane to Santa Fe, a day early." She took a big gulp of the wine and gently wiped her tears, her perfect manicure in full view. In spite of her current emotional state, she was an impressive beauty.

"Okay, now what exactly were they doing?" Caroline asked. "Maybe he was consoling her with a hug or something. I just can't imagine this."

"*Hug?* Caroline, this was a full-body embrace. They were kissing..." Diana's voice broke off into tears. "*My Jackson? Having an affair? How did this happen? How could this happen right under my nose?*"

Caroline put her arms around her friend and reassured her that there must be some mistake. This could not be happening. Next to her sister Julia and David, this was the longest, most solid marriage she knew. "Have you allowed for the fact that maybe what you saw wasn't what you think?"

"Are you *defending* him Caroline?" Diana challenged.

"Uh--no...okay - the man is a pig! He's dirt...he's...he's... Is that what you want to hear? Geez Diana, *this is Jackson!*" Caroline scrambled for a reasonable response. She found this whole scenario difficult to comprehend, yet she knew that at this moment there would be no reasoning with Diana. Her throat panged and she found herself in tears, too. She knew all too well how it felt to be in this situation.

"No one will believe this," said Diana, after a few more sips of wine. "And I'm not going to be the fool here."

"You are going to have to be very smart about this, Diana," warned Caroline. "Jackson is a public person and the last thing you need is a scandal."

"Right now, I don't care one iota about his public persona – I'm so angry," Diana said.

"Right! *Public schmublic*! He's a jerk! The man has clay feet!" Caroline chimed in, regardless of her doubts, and again she reiterated, "Honey, this is Jackson! I think I'm going to get us some coffee," she added. She noticed that their diction was getting a little sloppy. Wine on an empty stomach was not such a good idea. "I'll be right back."

As soon as Caroline left the room, Diana went into the bathroom to retouch her make up. After powdering the streaks made by her tears, she looked around the room. Candles all around the tub; *Nice touch, she thought*. A CD player; *Patsy Cline? Since when?* She opened the cabinet and saw that Frank's shaving kit was there; "*Hmmm*" she said out loud. As she passed by the walk-in closet, she peeked in. On the left side which had obviously been Frank's, Diana noticed Frank's boots, leather jacket and a guitar; *things she can't let go of, maybe?* Here she had been crying about her husband's idiocy, while Caroline was still mourning the death of her husband. Feeling a little confused, she thought – *Well, maybe it was the wine.*

Caroline returned with the coffee, and they spent an awkward moment in silence, searching for the best way to resume their painful conversation.

Diana spoke first. "I'm sorry...I'm so busy complaining about Jackson, I forgot that this must be hard to hear when you are still missing Frank so much. Listen, I saw Frank's..."

Caroline interrupted, "You *saw* Frank? I didn't think anyone else could see him but me...I mean..." Her voice trailed off, and she quickly drank more coffee.

"What I started to say was that I see that you still have so many of Frank's things still here," Diana said. "Not just the pictures, but the boots, the music...I understand this Caroline. Part of you thinks he may still want them when he returns. *"Wait - What did you mean? You can see him?"*

"You were in my closet?" Caroline asked.

"No, I was in the bathroom and walked by the closet, which was open," Diana answered. "I know you Caroline. You are probably trying your best to keep him here with you. We can talk about this another time if you like, when you're ready and we're both a little less emotional."

"Not now, Diana. Please not now. We're going to have a nice dinner with Marti, Kate, Siggy, Carmen and JB. I don't want to do this now."

"I understand," Diana said. She had always understood.

⊶❦⊷

In the late 1970's Caroline met and fell in love with one of the political activist leaders at UCLA. They were an on-again-off-again couple for two and a half years, until just after graduation day. Ric Roberts realized that his disillusionment with the government and the growing public apathy about the war in Vietnam should be turned into something more productive. He could stop being the angry activist and stop hurting Caroline, the person he loved the most. Ric was offered a job as the campaign manager for a candidate in the governor's race in North Carolina. When he confirmed his contract, he drove straight to Caroline and Marti's place and asked Caroline to marry him. They drove to Las Vegas, and the next day became husband and wife.

The newlyweds then moved to North Carolina, where Ric began to work the campaign for James B. Hunt, a bona fide progressive. At each event during the campaign, Hunt asked local ministers to give an invocation. At a formal fundraising dinner, Caroline was seated next to Diana, while their husbands shared the dais. Ric and Caroline were impressed by the eloquent Reverend Jackson Greene and the elegant Diana Greene. Diana invited them for a dinner date and took them on a tour of the Raleigh area.

Ric worked hard on the campaign and Hunt won. Fortunately, Hunt made Ric an offer and created a permanent position for him on his staff. Ric stayed with the governor until he became bored with Southern politics. After five years, he sought work elsewhere. Caroline worked for the city of Raleigh as a social worker until she gave birth to their first son, Brad. Reverend Jackson performed the baby's baptism at his church. Ric and Caroline were a family now and occasionally included church activities in their busy schedules. Although all four of them were incredibly busy with their careers, Diana, Jackson, Ric, and Caroline made a point of taking a break from Raleigh and finding a restaurant or concert to attend on a fairly regular basis. Diana and Jackson needed a night away from church people, and Caroline and Ric needed time away from politics.

Diana had always been impeccably dressed and always conducted herself gracefully. She also, always *"looked like a million dollars"* on a minister's salary, which in those days was not a fortune. Caroline once asked her how she always managed to look so perfect. Her surprising answer was that she was raised in the Deep South, and since both of her parents were professionals, she was often in the company of their colleagues who were mostly white people. In order to be taken seriously, they worked hard at never appearing like, *"poor black folks"*, for in their era they continually had to prove themselves.

During Diana's high school years, busing came into effect, nationally. Day after day, it was difficult to know who was a friend and who was an enemy. She believed she had to work harder, get better grades, look and *be perfect,* to be accepted. Although it was difficult to maintain such high standards, she thought carefully before she did or said anything. As a result, she developed great self-discipline and her own personal style. Diana learned to find value in herself and not to judge herself by the standards of others, but by the quality of her character and actions. Her great reward for her diligence was a college scholarship.

Diana and Jackson met during their first week at college and soon became a popular couple on campus. She was tall, slender and beautiful. In those days, she had what was known as the "*it*" factor.

Jackson may have been the great Reverend, but Diana was the great business manager. It was her idea for Jackson to begin a television ministry. And it worked. People loved him, and they loved him with their checkbooks.

By the late 1970's and early 1980's, Jackson and Diana were part of the newly visible "beautiful people" from the African-American community, who were now recognized nationally. Diana chose to stay behind the scenes, yet she was a full partner with Jackson in his ministry. They eventually had two beautiful daughters, neither of whom showed any interest in the ministry. The oldest daughter obtained a law degree and moved to San Francisco, and the youngest daughter became a ballerina with the Houston Ballet Company. It was difficult to think of Jackson without Diana, and vice versa. They were one of those couples that had purpose and a mission that fulfilled them both, and from all appearances, bonded them for life.

As Diana and Caroline grew closer, Diana confided some of the issues around running a sizeable church, including the never ending financial stress. Everyone *and his brother* had ideas as to how Jackson should direct the ministry. His only confidant was Diana. Early in his career, somewhat due to his friendship with Ric Roberts, he made a vow to himself, and Diana, to stay out of anything to do with politics.

By the time Caroline and Ric had marital problems, there were two sons in the Robert's family, Brad and Jarrod. Jackson counseled Ric and Diana offered Caroline a comforting, listening ear. Neither of the Greene's' wanted to see the Roberts family break up. Caroline's fury over some of Ric's choices left her feeling betrayed and abandoned. She eventually packed up the boys and returned to California, to seek her sister Julia's wisdom and nurturance. Caroline did not return to Raleigh. Diana hid her disappointment, but often sent supportive letters, never wanting to lose touch with Caroline.

When Caroline remarried, Diana was happy for her. She immediately accepted Caroline's first invitation to come to Angel-Fire for an annual friends retreat, and would by no means ever break from this company of friends.

Dinner for Five, Six or Seven

"It is not so much what's on the table that matters,
as what's on the chairs"

W.S. Gilbert

*D*iana settled into Bungalow #1 to freshen up before dinner. She decided it was best to turn off her cell phone for the night. She wanted to at least attempt to set her circumstances aside for a few hours and enjoy reuniting with friends. Diana knew that the salve that soothes a broken heart is often the company of a good friend.

Caroline assisted Carmen with the final details for the first feast of the retreat. Basically, that meant that Caroline, dressed in her western suede fringed skirt, leather boots and embroidered shirt, set the table, selected the wine and fluffed the flowers. She had arranged for three of the ten square tables in the dining room to be pushed together to make one long table for eight. Seven place settings, seven candles, seven small gifts.

Carmen was an outstanding cook and wholly territorial of *her* kitchen. This was one of her areas of expertise, and Caroline was glad to oblige. Carmen's specialty was simple, authentic regional dishes, both Native American and New Mexican. In an ordinary week, Carmen created a breakfast buffet for the AngelFire guests. They rarely served dinners for their guests at the Inn, as Frank thought it was best to encourage guests to patronize the local restaurants. Occasionally, for a special event, they would bring in a chef or recruit students from one of the culinary arts programs in Albuquerque. Carmen loved cooking for these annual retreats and planned her menus weeks in advance. Tonight's faire would start with Albóndigas soup, which consisted of tiny meatballs laced with mint in a broth and chopped fresh vegetables. The entrée was roasted chicken with wild sage bread stuffing and for the dessert, Natilla custard. For a perfect complement, bottles of a Santa Fe Riesling were placed on ice.

JB entered the dining room with an arm full of fir logs for the fireplace. He set them on the hearth and turned to Caroline. "I need to finish up some work in the barn. Do you mind if I skip this dinner?" he asked.

"You are the only man I know who would skip the chance to have six women fawn all over him. I heard them talking about you today...*this rugged, handsome man must have some brothers – right*?" she laughed. "You needn't be shy with these women JB; they love you. Oh, never mind, of course I won't mind, but you are staying in AngelFire at the house tonight – aren't you?"

JB sauntered over to Caroline and gave her one of his big bear hugs nearly knocking her off her feet. "Are you doin' okay?" he asked, not waiting for an answer. "Next week it'll be a year. It's still hard isn't it...for both of us? I've played that scene over in my head a thousand times to see if we could have done anything differently. Nothing comes, nothing at all."

"JB, I think he's okay with it." She whispered.

"I know he is. I still have those dreams. He knows everything, doesn't he? He knows we won't leave you alone here. Sometimes, I feel like he's..."

"He is, JB, he is," Caroline admitted. "Now go ahead and tend to the horses. Don't make me have to redo my makeup before dinner. I'll take a place setting off the table. Let's see now, that makes six."

Carmen stood under the archway of the butler's pantry, which was the server's walkway between the kitchen and dining room. She stood quietly, stirring something in a bowl and watching her husband and her closest friend; both still grieving. "Damn you Frank Amoroso, as long as you're still here, they suffer. Move on Frank, and let us move on too," she muttered. She returned to the kitchen, and then quietly slipped away to don an authentic Zuni beaded dress.

Marti and Siggy arrived first, together. Marti was dressed in casual black pants, sandals and a black silk blouse. Her African braids were pulled back and wrapped into themselves. Siggy wore a bright primary colored paisley caftan and a cherry red scarf in her multi-shades-of-blonde hair. She was jubilant and gregarious, as if that scene with her daughter just a few hours before had never happened.

"I brought a dessert," Siggy announced.

"Yippee," Marti mumbled.

"Shut-up...It is a simple caramel crème flan. It is really rather ordinary, except for..."

"I knew it, here it comes..." Marti teased. "The kohlrabi garnish – right?"

"Stop it, Marti." Caroline begged, half smiling.

"No, it is a sauce called 'Beautiful'. It's made with Grand Marnier and Courvoisier. After a few sips of this sauce everything and everybody seems beautiful! Even I'm beautiful, dang it!"

Their laughter was interrupted by Diana's entrance. She was dressed in fine white linen from head to toe and was wearing the intricate Navaho silver and turquoise jewelry she had purchased during Indian Market days in Santa Fe.

For a little diversion, Diana and Jackson had stayed on in Santa Fe for a few days after Frank's funeral. They didn't know Frank very well, but they had a long history with Caroline, and Diana was hesitant about leaving the state too soon. One of those nights, Caroline's oldest son Brad joined Jackson and Diana for dinner and a little reminiscing. He was a North Carolina born son, and two years older than Jackson and Diana's first-born daughter.

❦

"Well Diana Greene, I didn't know you were here," Siggy said charging in for a hug. "How's the famous Reverend Greene?"

Caroline quickly interrupted, "Has anyone seen Kate?"

"Marti, you didn't tell me Dr. Kate was here too. This *is* a party!" Siggy chimed in.

"She never answered her wake-up call. I have a note from one of the staff, who took a message from bungalow #3, that says '*See you in the morning*'," Carmen said, as she entered the room carrying a tray of jicama juliennes and a variety of guacamoles, and looking dazzling in her Zuni beaded dress and long black braided hair, "I think she's still asleep."

"Look at you!" You look gorgeous!" Siggy exclaimed.

"Let's let Katie be," Marti advised. "She'll be fine tomorrow."

"Okay, I'll take away her place setting – now we're five. Who'd like some wine?" offered Caroline.

The conversation was a catch-up fest for the recipes and new ventures of Siggy and a lending of support for Marti's latest musical endeavors. Diana volunteered nothing, and Caroline just kept pouring wine. Carmen and her significant culinary talents were the real stars of the evening. After receiving the accolades and praises from her guests, Carmen responded, "You don't understand ladies – this is just plain home cooking."

"Don't underrate what you have done tonight, Carmen. We appreciate all your efforts. Because you see, we've all known

Caroline for a very long time, and we would not be eating this well if she were the chef," said Marti.

Ignoring Marti's remark Caroline said, "Well then, how about if you open your little gifts?" The gifts were crystal paperweights with the AngelFire insignia in silver, suspended within. Caroline had one made for Frank the year before, and it was still on his desk. He liked it so much he had them made by the dozen, and saved them for special guests. They were none more special than this group on this night.

Frank knew of Caroline's shortcomings in the kitchen, too. While the Inn was being built, he casually mentioned this to JB as they worked side by side. When the hiring of the staff began, JB reluctantly asked Frank to consider interviewing his wife, Carmen, since he thought she would impress the Amorosos' with her culinary skills. His reluctance was due to the possible strain that could develop when a husband and wife work together. JB invited Frank and Caroline to dinner at their home, and the four enjoyed a grand dinner of regional dishes. By the end of the evening, Frank and Caroline discovered that Carmen was experienced in several areas and that she could become a real asset to the AngelFire Inn. She was the liaison to the city of Taos for the Pueblo, and had produced community events to promote both. Frank made her an offer that night and after a few days of lengthy discussions with her husband, she accepted.

Carmen and Caroline were more than compatible coworkers. With their shared efforts on behalf of the success of the Inn, they became good friends. All four worked hard to build a regular guest base for the Inn, and each had specific areas of expertise that contributed to its success.

Caroline was impressed by Carmen's abilities with the children who were guests at the Inn. She knew that Carmen took more pleasure playing with the children in the craft and game room than in any other part of her work.

During the first women's retreat, Carmen prepared the wonderful food the group so very much enjoyed. By the second year, Caroline decided Carmen should share the fun with her dear friends and included her as a co-host of this party of women. She naturally blended in as the newest and very welcome addition to the company of friends.

⚜

Each of the women had drunk enough wine to bravely sample Siggy's desert. More laughter and wine...was just what they needed. They were having such a delightful time they did not notice the bell ringing in the lobby. After the fourth ring, the new arrivals found their own way to the dining room.

Nicole and her guest Paula, interrupted the party with a "Hel-loooo...is anybody here sober?"

"Niki!" Caroline exclaimed as she jumped up to hug her. "I wasn't expecting you until tomorrow or the next day. Sit down and introduce your friend. We have plenty of food and lots more wine." As Caroline set two more places, Nicole moved around the table, introducing her friend Paula, who oddly enough looked like her *separated-at-birth* twin. Both women were in traveling jeans and wore similar colorful knit tops. Paula was more reserved than the somewhat inebriated women who were now a little loud and giddy, while Nicole jumped right into the conversations, just as loud, but not so giddy.

Carmen had scheduled two of the AngelFire staff to attend to the service and cleanup of this reunion dinner, so that she and Caroline could relax and enjoy their guests. Carmen was pleased as she watched Caroline laugh more during this evening than she had in months. She slipped out of the room for a moment to ask the staff to get extra linens and to deliver the baggage left in the reception area to Bungalow #5. Silently, Carmen allowed herself a moment to sense her accomplishments for the evening and her value to Caroline.

Although Nicole and Paula were enjoying themselves, they were weary from their long drive from Chicago. Caroline glanced over at Nicole, her former sister-in law, and noticed that she was completely comfortable in this group of women, most of whom were at least ten years her senior. No doubt she and her friend Paula had rallied around some judicious cause in Chicago that bonded yet another friend for life.

Nicole was Caroline's sister-in-law from her marriage to Ric Roberts. Devastated by Ric and Caroline's divorce, Nicole became the liaison to the Roberts family and transportation for Caroline's children to all the Roberts family affairs and extra visits with Grandma Roberts. She made a promise to Caroline's sons, Brad and Jarrod, that she would do all she could to keep them close to the Roberts family, particularly since their father's frequent travels often kept him in Washington, DC. Nicole stayed in California until the boys were in high school and able to drive their own cars. She was a remarkable organizer and was a volunteer for the crisis du jour in Los Angeles. She had little time for dating but was seldom alone.

Nicole and Paula were fed and their wine glasses filled and refilled, and for an hour or so, their exhaustion was nearly forgotten. Their laughter had weaved its way into the fabric of the evening.

As the effects of the wine began to set in for Siggy, she asked Diana, "So how is the great Reverend Greene? We watch him on TV every now and then and his audience looks bigger each time. My sons love him! You must be so proud."

Diana hesitated, then answered, "He's fine."

Marti, picking up on the hesitation, said, "Oh he's fine all right, and I'll bet you get letters every week from all kinds of good Christian women who think he's *fine*."

Caroline responded protectively with, "Diana stopped looking at that kind of mail years ago."

Diana added, "Sometimes lonely people do or say strange things or write letters that we consider sort of sad."

"Must be hard living with such celebrity and having an image to protect," Carmen added.

"*Image?* You're right, Carmen. Right now I'm here to decide if it's worth it," Diana confessed, with a single tear rolling down her cheek. "Sometimes it's harder than it should be. The good Reverend may have done it this time. It may just be too damn hard."

The table was silenced for a second, in a collective gasp... *Did Diana just swear?*

Marti spoke first, "Nothing and no one is perfect all the time, for anybody. Public life is just too demanding. It's okay for you to be real with all of us. We're not going to remember any of this in the morning anyway."

"Thank you, I...I...I think my husband might be having an affair," she whimpered.

"Wwhhhaaaaatt?" was the unanimous reply.

"Now we don't know anything for sure, yet," Caroline warned.

"Please God, don't let this be true for her," Siggy said, with tears now rolling down her face, too. All the women were shocked and distraught, but Siggy appeared more emotional than the others.

Marti asked, "Now, why are you crying?"

"Look, I know how hard it was for her to tell us this. To confess that your heart is breaking is humiliating. Oh, Diana, I hope this is some kind of awful misunderstanding," Siggy said, her voice breaking into a moan.

"Are you okay?" Marti asked Siggy. The now mutual concern, shifted toward Siggy.

"Well, no, not exactly...you see I have a little confession to make too," Siggy sniveled. "You weren't all present when my daughter brought me here today. She was so mad at me I'm lucky she didn't drop me off over a cliff."

Carmen quickly found a box of tissues and set them on the table and all seven women took one. "Well," she asked, "What happened?"

"I was visiting her at their newly remodeled vacation home in Durango, Colorado and was making some candy with my granddaughters, and I had a little accident. One thing led to another, and then the kids were screaming, and by the time the volunteer fire department came...well... the kitchen was destroyed."

"Wwhhhaaaaatt?" Marti replied along with all the others "Oh my God!" "Was anyone hurt?"

"No one was hurt, but I'm not sure my daughter will ever speak to me again," She sobbed.

The tissues were passed around again, while Caroline and Marti tried to console both Siggy and Diana.

"Well, while we all seem to be going to confession tonight...I have something to confess too," said Marti. "I wasn't going to tell anyone, but what the heck, I might as well."

All eyes turned to Marti, and a deep inhale around the table allowed for a brief moment of anticipation.

"Are you all right? You're not sick are you?" Carmen blurted.

Caroline wiped her eyes, and asked, "What is it?"

"Erik found me on the Internet...uh, well, we kind of found each other," Marti divulged.

"You found your son on the Internet? Doing what?" asked Siggy, as she wiped away her tears.

"No, not my son, my son's *father*," she admitted.

"Wwhhhaaaaatt?" *It was Siggy's turn.* Caroline was silent and the others were aghast.

"Wasn't he a POW or something in Vietnam?" Siggy asked.

"No, I lied about that...He's an architect in Sweden...There, I said it! He's alive and an architect living in Stockholm. I've lied about him for nearly thirty years – and – I'm sorry," declared Marti. "I'm sorry that I lied to all of you...and to my son Erik,

Jr. .... I don't know how I am ever going to clean this up," Marti wailed.

Caroline burst into tears and buried her head on Carmen's shoulder. She knew how enormous the burden of living that lie has been for Marti.

By now the room was full of weeping women, so Carmen got up and pulled the wine off the table. Caroline was hugging Diana; Siggy was consoling Marti; and Nicole was apologizing to Paula for a night of red nosed, bleary eyed, sorrowful, weeping women.

"Anything you want to come clean with while we're at it Caroline?" Carmen asked, hoping Caroline would now confess her own secret ....

Caroline took a deep breath and answered, "Well, okay...I...yes, uh...I do. I don't want any of you to be alarmed or anything .... but I have seen Frank recently."

"Frank's not dead either?" Siggy shrieked.

"Yes, he's still dead...*but* he's come back recently and is trying to tell me something. I talk to him, but I haven't gotten what he is trying to tell me, quite yet," Caroline mumbled. The unanimous silence that followed was not the reply she expected.

Then, all of a sudden, everyone spoke at once...."Is he here right now? Is he in this room? Oh my God, is AngelFire haunted by of Frank Amoroso? Is he here, NOW?"

Carmen wrapped her arms around Caroline and cried with her. "I knew he was back. Both you and my husband have been acting so secretive for the past month or two.... "

The room was filled with tears, tissues and the blathering of weeping women, each one more sorry for the other.

Nicole stood up and hit the side of her glass with a spoon. And in her husky, raspy, sexy voice, said, "Before we all go to our rooms and cry ourselves to sleep tonight, I have a confession, too. I am speaking for Paula and myself."

With a red nose and bleary eyes, Siggy said, "I don't know if I can take any more sadness tonight. Nicole, honey – do you at least have your health?"

Nicole continued..."Well here it is...after eleven years with Chicago Unified, Paula and I got fired this week. Both of us." Before she could go any further, Caroline spoke up.

"I am so sorry," Caroline cried. "Don't worry about a thing, either of you. You can both stay here while you find other jobs. Why did they fire you?"

"Well - they have their rules and policies... and they said they couldn't have a gay couples working at the same school."

"Okay, so...what does that have to do with you?" asked Siggy.

"Uh....after eleven years, they just figured out you were gay?" Marti asked.

"Wait a minute Marti, - _I_ just figured out _I_ was gay!" Nicole snapped.

"Uh...Well, uh...hmmm...uh what?" Mixed mumbling was not the reply she expected.

In perfect synchronicity, Siggy, Marti and Carmen said, *"You just figured out you were gay?"*

One Last Confession

"The most beautiful discovery true friends make is that they can grow separately without growing apart."

- Elizabeth Foley

Sometime after ten the next morning, Caroline trudged down to the kitchen. JB was alone sitting in the breakfast nook sipping coffee and writing on some paper. "Congratulations," he said without looking at her. "I think you are the first survivor to surface."

Caroline groaned. She opened the refrigerator and just stood there.

"It's on the counter," he said, still not looking at her.

Caroline turned toward the counter, placed a wobbly hand around a glass of red liquid, stared at it, then brought it up to her nose for a sniff. "Do I want to know what this is?"

"Nope," he answered. "Zuni cure...I've left wake up calls for your friends. Breakfast will be served at eleven-thirty today. I'm cooking."

She turned to ask about Carmen, but on second thought - *uh, maybe not.*

"Don't even ask," he said, knowing exactly what was on her mind.

At eleven-thirty, seven women still in their AngelFire terry robes, and large dark sunglasses, sat at the dining room table, heads in hands. No one said much more than a light groan, which was supposedly interpreted as "Good morning," - which was responded to with reciprocal laments.

Carmen was the first to speak. "He is going to make us eat something, which is probably a good thing, but I feel I must warn you..."

The warning was interrupted by a fully rested, bubbly, *top-of-the-mornin'-to-ya-Kate.* "Good morning!" she said jubilantly. I've been out for a long walk this morning and it is a glorious day and ...hey, what the heck happened to all of you? Nicole! Wow, when did you get in? You look terrible – Geez, what happened here? Diana! – Uh, Diana? Okay, what's going on here?"

"Could you tone it down Katie?" Marti asked, cupping her hands over her ears.

"You missed quite a night," Caroline started. "I don't even know where to begin."

"Coffee?" asked the host. JB poured New Mexico Pinon coffee in each cup around the room and gave instructions for breakfast. "Okay ladies, since I am your chef this morning, I decided to make New Mexico omelets – Zuni style. I promise...you are all going to feel much better."

"Mea Culpa," Carmen whispered to her husband.

"I'm starved!" said Kate. "Isn't anybody going to tell me anything?"

"After about four more cups of coffee," Siggy answered.

"Well, while we're all waiting for our food, I have a confession to make," Kate said, beaming like the first ray of sunshine on a much too cloudy day.

Seven robed women, still in sunglasses, held their breath and turned to hear her news.

"Last night, while I was getting ready to come over here for dinner with all of you, my phone rang and it was Robbie Collicci. He invited me to meet him for dinner...and I went! I didn't think anyone would mind. Anyway, I haven't been out with a man on a real date in what seems like forever and...well, I couldn't resist! I really like this man, and he is actually going to pick me up again later and take me to Taos for another date and...and.why isn't anybody saying anything?"

Caroline spoke first, "We love you Katie...we are all happy for you....but we are in a lot of pain right now. Trust me; you don't want a hug from me this morning." Each woman "ughed" in agreement.

Kate, who was utterly perplexed, glanced around the table.

Before she could respond, JB looking rather proud of himself, announced, "Breakfast is served." He and an assistant brought out plates with omelets, fried potatoes and baskets of sopapillas and honey.

Seven women, still wearing their sunglasses stared at their plates; each only having the courage to pick up a fork, but the eighth, Kate, took a bite. "This is amazing," she said as she tasted the food.

Carmen drew up the courage to be next. She took one bite and said nothing. The remaining women in their sunglasses took a bite of the omelet and the gasping began. Each grabbed for her water until Carmen said "Not the water! Not the water! Grab the sopapillas and the honey!" She demonstrated slathering the honey inside the fried puffed pastry and ate it. Six women in their sunglasses followed suit.

One woman with her bright, smiling Irish face, said, "My food's not hot. Why do you suppose yours is?"

Now What?

"I get by with a little help from my friends."

- John Lennon

By seven-thirty that night, each of the women had to some extent, recovered. A very light dinner was followed with a plan to meet at the fire pit, and everyone but Caroline arrived on time. Siggy had spent the afternoon baking and offered up her latest concoction of raspberry avocado swirls.

"Well they're pretty," said Paula and Nicole, almost in unison.

Diana covered her white tone-on-tone silk caftan with three napkins before she took a bite. "They look like Christmas," she said, reserving a comment on the taste. "Are they an hors d'oeuvres or a sweet?"

Siggy declined to answer. Everyone tasted one, and everyone actually ate the whole swirl. *Things are looking up!* she thought.

Marti heard the music first and said, "Are we hearing Patsy Cline again?"

"It's coming from Caroline's window," said Carmen. "It seems to be her theme song these days."

"She's up there with Frank," said Diana. "I saw some of his things, when I was in her apartment yesterday. She plays his music and conjures him up, I guess. Do you think it's her imagination?"

"He's trying to tell her something," Kate added. "He's come back for a reason."

"I'm not going to ask how you know that," said Nicole.

Kate ignored the comment. She was accustomed to skepticism about her intuitive abilities.

"We have to help her with this," said Marti. "Carmen, does she do this often?"

"Daily. Ladies, my friend and my husband would love to have Frank Amoroso right back here at AngelFire. I'm just as worried about JB as I am Caroline. Too many secrets. My husband feels such guilt for Frank's death. They were working on projects together that Caroline and I knew nothing about. She and JB are both still mourning deeply. My husband is so withdrawn, and Caroline does exactly what you think she is doing; right now as we hear that music."

"My grandmother swore that my grandpa was with her for years. We all believed her. He died suddenly, and we all just felt he didn't want to leave her alone," said Paula.

"That also means that you don't go on with your life," said Siggy. "I held on to the belief that my husband was going to come to his senses, leave that young girl he ran off with, and return to me and the kids. I'd forgive him and we'd put our family back together. I wasted ten years of my life, holding on to the past. We can't let Caroline do this for very long."

"He will go away when she understands the message," said Kate.

"Thank you Madam Zara," said Marti.

Caroline met JB outside of the front entrance and together they headed for the fire pit. The circle of friends spoke softly as they watched them approach. JB was carrying an armload of pine logs. When they reached the gathering, JB stacked the extra logs near the fire and turned to speak to Carmen. "We have to go...they need you tonight."

"Okay, I'll get my bag," Carmen said. She quickly rose and gave seven quick hugs and apologies around the fire pit. JB was sharing the problems of the coming meeting, when they soon realized Caroline had followed them.

"Wait, is there something wrong? Can I help?" she asked.

"Trouble at the high school again," answered JB. "We'll be back tonight."

"Call me if you need anything," she said. Then, she returned to her friends and said, "Okay, ladies let the good times roll!"

"Whoa, Annie Oakley livin' out here in the Wild West, I'm not sure I've got an ounce of good times in me to roll tonight," said Marti.

"I do!" bragged Kate. "And I'm going to see Robbie Collicci again, later on tonight."

"We're happy for you Katie, all of us, really" said Caroline. "Robbie's a terrific guy. He's been a good friend and great help to me this year. I don't think I could have managed all this without him. He and Frank became very close. We really lucked out finding him."

"Finding him? I thought Robbie told me he'd known Frank all his life. He also told me that you have to come in and see him. It's time Caroline, for you to know where you stand. He told me you have nothing to worry about, but that there are things you need to be aware of," said Kate.

"Okay, you're starting to sound like my sister, Julia," Caroline answered.

"Actually, we all feel it's time for you to take charge, Caroline," said Diana. Nods were followed by murmurs of agreement.

"Wait," said Kate. "Before you get the wrong idea... You know we love you and we believe that Frank is here. Really here...He has a message for you honey. Do you have any idea what it is?"

"Not yet," Caroline answered. "At first I thought he just wanted to be with me, but I know there is more. He's trying to say something to me... I just can't tell what it is. Look, I know you think I'm a little crazy living way out here away from everything and everyone; please remember...*we were happy*, and I've grown to love it here. It's been twelve good years. Once I wanted to see the whole world, and now I don't think that's ever going to happen. I really am content here."

"Are you having sex with him up there?" asked Nicole.

While the circle gasped, Caroline gathered herself and said, "My sex life is as private as yours."

"I knew it!" said Marti. "And you're right Caroline, so we don't want details...it's just comforting to know that there *is* sex on the other side."

"Woo-hoo! There is always hope!" Siggy said half laughing, while the others were fully laughing.

"I'll help you figure this out," Kate said. "You know, I'm pretty good at this."

"Once again, thank you Madame Zara," added Marti. "Have a raspberry avocado swirl...you'll love it!"

"Could we not do this now?" Caroline said. "Siggy, tell us what's new with your snack business."

"Well, you all know that I am now the owner of a registered, licensed business, known as 'Siggy's Sweets & Snacks'. And as usual, I entered a couple of contests this year. My Pizza Popcorn actually took third place at a food fair in Van Nuys. But the last time I went to the movies, they had a new set of powdered flavorings to sprinkle on your popcorn, so I guess that idea is already taken. The flavorings were from McKormicks; you know, the spice people. I can't compete with the big guys. I know I'll come up with something. Billions of dollars are spent on snacks each year. It's part of the American economy. I just need to figure out something that hasn't been done yet."

"Siggy, snacks are usually considered junk foods, although the world probably isn't going to stop eating them. Can you focus on something healthy? You could play off the First Lady's programs for healthy children and maybe even pick up some contracts from the local school systems," offered Diana.

"Ever the business woman," said Caroline.

"When you have a product, maybe I could help you with a business plan and proposal. You have certainly been creative. I would gladly give you a little business advice," Diana added.

"Thank you Diana. Just when I was thinking I should give up; with the fire happening and all."

"Siggy, what *exactly* happened?" asked Marti. "Have you heard from Sherry?"

"No, she won't be talking to me for some time, at least until she has her kitchen back. I don't really know *exactly* what happened. I was making some candy for the girls and you know how hot that gets...I was feeling kind of dizzy, and then well, I'm not sure what happened. All I know is that the next thing I knew there was smoke everywhere. I panicked and got the girls out of the house, and then tried to find a neighbor to help. But in those mountains the houses are far apart. When I went back into the house, the smoke was pretty thick. That's when Sherry pulled up in the driveway. She used her cell phone to dial 911, and she asked me if it was her new kitchen that was on fire. I didn't speak and she didn't say anything much to me. She cried, and then got really angry. Actually I think *'went ballistic'* is a better description."

"Siggy, you said you were dizzy. Did you faint?" asked Kate.

"I'm not sure. I'd been having some bad headaches for a few days."

"Does Sherry know this?" asked Marti. "I think she should..."

Kate interrupted, "Siggy, we need to figure out why you fainted. Are you still having headaches now?"

"It's just a little headache. I'm fine."

"Why don't you come with me? We'll go back to my bungalow and check you out a little," said Kate.

"No, we won't," said Siggy, "*I'm fiiiiine.*"

"Ok, then...tomorrow," said Caroline, insistently.

"Can I say something about your snack business?" asked Nicole. Without waiting for an answer she continued. "Madison Avenue targets kids for nearly everything. Why not something for women – who are on diets? You'd pique our curiosity, and if the snacks are good, and less than 100 calories, you'd get our appreciation, too! I'd love a dessert that I don't have to feel guilty about. Of course, that is until we get to Thanksgiving, then all diets are off! I want one of everything! I love pies!"

Agreeable laughter spun round the circle.

"Pattie's Pies just went out of business," Siggy sighed. "I don't think one can make a living making pies anymore. I used to be good at them, too. Remember my mother's special crust, Marti? Okay...I'll think about something healthy for dieters or healthy for kids." Siggy had acquiesced, and was frosted with discouragement. She'd put years into these projects and now her best supporters, *and guinea pigs*, were still asking her to try something new. Her head hurt.

Caroline realized it was time to change the subject, and said, "Marti, would you be willing to play some of your music for us?"

"Sure, I'd be happy to," she answered.

"Okay ladies," said Caroline. "Let us embark upon a journey to the AngelFire Performing Arts Center."

Marti led the way, while Caroline dowsed the fire. Everyone always enjoyed the music room. It brought joy and laughter to both the players and their audiences. It was Frank's idea. He created the "Music in the Mountains" studio and found plenty of used instruments which provided a great time for AngelFire guests. He added a sound system, and JB built a small stage for family concerts. Many memories of good times filled this room, and its essence brought a lighthearted energy to Caroline's circle of friends.

Caroline fiddled with the sound system, adding the traditional unprofessional trill from a microphone, and then proceeded to announce: "Ladies and Ladies, the AngelFire Inn is proud to present to you this evening, a pianist extraordinaire whose talents will dazzle you as she plays...for the first time in public. Ms. Marti Westerlund will perform her latest composition, soon to be featured with the Pacific Symphony. *Applause, applause, applause!*"

A note of seriousness washed over Marti's face. Then, with a side wink to Caroline, she hit the keyboard and broke out in song...

You shake my nerves and you rattle my brain
Too much love drives a girl insane
You broke my will
But what a thrill
Goodness gracious great balls of fire!
I laughed at love cause I thought it was funny
But you came along and moooooved me honey
I've changed my mind
This love is fine
Goodness gracious great balls of fire!

With screams of laughter the rest of women sang along...

Kiss me baby
Mmmm feels good
Hold me baby
Well I want to love you like a lover should
You're fine, so kind
Got to tell this world that you're mine mine mine mine
I chew my nails and I twiddle my thumbs
I'm real nervous but it sure is fun
C'mon baby, you drive me crazy
Goodness gracious great balls of fire!

Marti thrilled her audience, who quickly rose to join the fun. Nicole jumped on the drum set and arranged the next beat. Paula picked up the lead guitar. Diana clutched the tambourine, and Kate and Siggy each seized a microphone. With a whisper to Nicole and Paula, Kate led with her rendition of...

I've been cheated
Been mistreated
When will I be loved
Then Siggy chimed in on the second verse........
I've been put down

I've been pushed 'round
When will I be loved

When I find a new man
That I want for mine
He always breaks my heart in two
It happens every time

Oh, I've been cheated
Been mistreated
When will I be loved
When will I be loved
Tell me, when will I be loved.

The soft hearted souls of Kate and Siggy really had experienced the truth of these lyrics, but both were good enough sports to just enjoy the song.

Diana was ready for her solo, and the two country songsters stepped aside and said, "Ladies and Ladies, for your listening pleasure...we present to you our very own Supreme, Miss Diana!! *Applause, applause, applause!*"... Diana drew her shoulders up and whispered ever so softly into the microphone, "Thank you, I love you. I love each and every one of you...." Then she took a deep sultry breath and sang...with Siggy and Kate as her backup singers...

No wind, (no wind) no rain, (no rain)
Nor winter's cold
Can stop me, babe (oh, babe) baby (baby)
If you're my goal
No wind, no rain
Can stop me, babe
If you wanna go

I know, I know you must follow the sun
Wherever it leads
But remember

If you should fall short of your desires
Remember life holds for you one guarantee
You'll always have me

And if you should miss my love
One of these old days
If you should ever miss the arms
That used to hold you so close, or the lips
That used to touch you so tenderly
Just remember what I told you
The day I set you free

Ain't no mountain high enough
Ain't no valley low enough (say it again)
Ain't no river wide enough
To keep me from you babe

And all joined in the last chorus...
Ain't no mountain high enough
Ain't no valley low enough (say it again)
Ain't no river wide enough
To keep me from getting you babe...

In the midst of the merriment, no one noticed that Caroline had left the room. Her six friends were belting out their songs and having a *blast*! Suddenly Caroline appeared at the top of the stairs with a bass guitar that exploded in a riff from Deep Purple's "Smoke on the Water". A gust of hysterical laughter swept the room as each took their instruments. Paula's lead guitar rang in, with Caroline repeating the riffs. Marti synchronized chords to match them. Nicole pounded the drums, and Diana shook the tambourine for all it was worth. Kate and Siggy prepared to step up to the microphones. They each took a deep breath and instead said, "Does anyone know the lyrics to this?"

Suddenly the doors burst open and everyone froze. JB said "What's going on in here? Oh, uh...Caroline? We heard the loud music, and I thought some kids got in here and..."

Carmen interrupted him and said, "Come on JB, let's dance. Rock on, girls!"

And the band played on.

About thirty feet away, outside a window, stood a specter of light in the outline of a man. It could not remain still, yet it was barely noticeable and...*it roared with laughter that echoed into the night.*

JB

"When you help someone up a hill,
You get closer to the top
Yourself"

Anonymous

All musicians and singers came to the breakfast table with a smile. They were *pretty darn proud* of themselves for the previous night's performances. All emotional barriers had melted, returning them to the true depth of their friendships. Each originally thought she had come to comfort her friend in mourning, but instead each had revealed her own crossroads and vulnerabilities. No one suspected they would be dealing with seven crises in one week, but who better to help than lifelong friends?

Plans were made for a day trip to Taos for lunch, shopping, and the annual tour of the Pueblo*. Carmen volunteered to drive the van. Caroline elected to stay behind, and Nicole asked Paula to go on the excursion without her.

About eleven, Caroline and Nicole waved a caring send-off to their friends, and as they turned toward the Inn, Caroline asked, "Would you like to take a walk to the lake with me?"

"Yes, I would like to talk to you. Let me get my hiking shoes on, and I'll meet you in the kitchen," Nicole responded.

Caroline went to the kitchen and found JB making more coffee. "Do you have a minute to talk?" she asked.

In JB's own quiet way, he nodded "*yes*".

"I know that Carmen has told you by now that Frank has returned, and I feel he is trying to tell me something...Are you seeing him too, JB?"

"No, I don't see him, but there are times when I feel like he is in the room..." started JB, "nearby, just watching me...I talk to him and ask him if there is something he wants me to do, but he doesn't answer me."

"What he wants you to do about what?" asked Caroline.

"About AngelFire, and you, and some of the projects we were working on for my people."

"What else could he want you to do? You do so much here JB. How could you possibly do more? Do you think I am wrong to keep the Inn going?"

"No, I don't. We all love this place and besides this, what else would we do? Carmen loves it here, too. We've both been happier here than at any other place either of us has ever worked. When we were younger, we sure never thought we could work together, but we've built something good here. If we could get the Inn back to being as busy as it was before Frank died, I think we'd all be happy. It would be a good tribute to Frank, too. The four of us accomplished a lot together. He was a businessman with a good heart, and he was very generous to Carmen and me. I don't think we would be this happy anywhere else."

"Most of our guests came year after year and many of them loved Frank. Maybe they think it would be too sad to come back here. Maybe they think we're shrouded in black, or worse, they know that Frank is still here and are and are afraid of ghosts!" Caroline said, half-jokingly.

"We'll just have to find new people, start doing some new advertising or something. We could start over and rebuild a group of regulars again. It would be good for all of us," said JB.

"If AngelFire is what you really want, Caroline...Is it? Do you know yet what you want to do? I'm sorry – here I've been going on about how much I love AngelFire, without even knowing how you really feel or what you want. Maybe you don't love it as much without Frank."

"First I have to see if the AngelFire Inn can afford to keep going. We have been avoiding reality here...me, most of all. Robbie says we have nothing to worry about financially, but my sister Julia, bless her heart, is probably right. Fortunately or unfortunately, she usually is. We've been working with half the amount of guests, so we can't possibly be making any money. But if we still have reserves, then I guess we'll try to rebuild our guest base. I don't have any idea what else I would do, either. Is there anything else I should do ...or should know about, JB?"

"Caroline, if it's true that you are seeing Frank, will you tell him something?" JB said, while avoiding her question.

"Of course, JB, what is it?"

"Will you tell him I'm sorry? I'm so sorry that I ...." The Rock-of-Gibraltar, stone-faced JB Robles dissolved into quiet, deeply remorseful tears. "...I couldn't save him."

Caroline threw her arms around JB's neck and wept with her guilt-stricken friend. "We all tried JB, all of us. Carmen and I tried to help, too. I don't know what else we could have done. I don't know how to let him go, JB," she sobbed. "Maybe he knows how much we miss him. Maybe that's why he's back. Maybe he misses us too. Do you think that's possible?"

They broke their embrace and stood in silence. Both of them wiped their eyes and tried to regain their composure.

"Nicole is on her way over here to go for a walk to the lake. I need to go wash my face. Will you have someone cover the phones for me?" she said, as she tried to dry her eyes, which were still brimming with tears.

"Sure," he said clearing his throat. "Caroline, there's something else."

Caroline looked wide-eyed at JB, hoping he hadn't been holding back more information. "What is it JB?"

"Sorry about that breakfast yesterday. Carmen said I over did it," he confessed.

At the top of the stairs, stood a specter of light, unseen for the light coming through the window. It remained still and...*it wept for them.*

JB Robles was working in construction, building a grand casino just outside of Albuquerque, and managing a crew of installers for the new gaming equipment. As each piece was uncrated, Frank Amoroso, representing the manufacturer, inspected the equipment and approved it before installation. Frank had noticed the hardworking supervisor Robles and was impressed by the way he spoke to his crew. This man with an imposing stature was a gentle lion, skillfully training his crew at every step. Frank was confident the supervisor's style would guarantee a successful outcome for everyone.

At the time, Frank had already broken ground on AngelFire and was in the process of building the foundations.

One day while JB was dismissing his crew for a lunch break, Frank invited him out to lunch. JB agreed to go, and they enjoyed a hamburger at a nearby café called "The Stove". Frank asked JB a lot of questions, and JB's answers revealed his extensive construction experience. He told JB that there was a project in northeastern New Mexico, which he would like to show him. At the time, home for Carmen and JB was near the Zuni Pueblo, just outside of Gallup, in the northwestern part of the state. Frank gave JB his card and asked him to think about it. Meanwhile, they retained a casual friendship with weekly lunches. JB eventually

spoke of his wife, their struggles and disappointment in a child-
less marriage, and Frank revealed that he was getting serious
about a social worker he was dating and was preparing for the
"big question" for the first time in his confirmed bachelor's life.

When the casino was in the final finishing stages, just before
the grand opening, Frank once again asked JB to take a look at
his project. Nearing the completion of a job, JB had to consider
all his options. So, he agreed to drive up and take a look at Frank's
project. Within a month, JB was on board. Carmen found a house
and work in Taos, and they started a new life together. After a
month on the job, Frank took his new project manager to lunch.
He spoke of future plans for the AngelFire Inn and offered him
a permanent position. He wanted JB to help recruit and manage the future staff. JB discussed the opportunity with Carmen,
realizing that it could be the beginning of a new life, one which
neither of them had ever thought possible.

When JB officially accepted the job, Frank was delighted. His
first response was, "Perfect, everything is perfect!"

"Why is everything so perfect, Frank?" asked JB.

"Because," he answered. "Last night she said 'Yes'!"

⚜

*Taos Pueblo is the only living Native American commu-
nity designated both a World Heritage Site by UNESCO and a
National Historic Landmark. The multi-storied adobe buildings
have been continuously inhabited for over 1000 years.}

Nicole

"The real voyage of discovery consists not in seeking new landscapes, but in having new eyes."

- Marcel Proust

N icole walked into the kitchen talking..."Sorry, I'm late, I was talking to my mother. I uh...Oh JB, sorry, have you seen Caroline?"

"She'll be down in a minute. She just went upstairs. She said you're walking to the lake."

"I'm ready, Nicole," called Caroline from the staircase. She descended quickly and walked straight over to JB, throwing her arms around his neck. "We're not guilty," she whispered in his ear. Overcome by the tender feelings within, he was unable to respond.

"Okay, let's go Nicole." Caroline armed with water bottles, a blanket, and a bundle of snacks, led the way to a path marked with a sign that said *"Serenity – This Way"*. They walked in silence for a few minutes, listening to the sounds of the birds and the crackle of the scampering squirrels. Rays of the morning sum poked through the canopy of trees and warmed their faces. "I'm so glad you're here," Caroline said softly. "I'm also really pleased that you didn't panic at getting fired. I intend to help you in any way I can."

"Thanks, Caroline. Paula and I both are very grateful. We'd like to stay here to figure out our next step. We will have to return to Chicago soon, though. There's the apartment, the bank accounts, you understand – the loose ends we'll have to take care of.

I spoke to my mother and she wants me to come back to California, which I would rather not do. By the way, she wants you to come for a visit, too," said Nicole in her deep, throaty voice. Her distinctive voice was often perceived by others, particularly men, as an exceedingly attractive quality, but one which Nicole never really appreciated. This was one area where there was no resemblance to Paula. As demonstrated the night before, Paula could sing, beautifully...Nicole could not.

"Maybe I'll go to Southern California in the winter. There is so much of my life there. My sons, Julia, of course Marti and Siggy and then there's Lila, your mom – it's a long list." They came to the edge of a stand of aspens and watched a great blue heron land to join another near the edge of the lake. "We surely don't see these very often," Caroline whispered "They must be just stopping over." She deftly moved closer, then spread the blanket and motioned for Nicole to join her. Caroline handed her a bottle of water and opened one for herself. She laid out peaches and almonds from a plastic container. Handing Nicole a juicy peach and a napkin, she said, "I'm happy you stayed behind this morning. I've wanted to talk with you.

I've known you since you were a young girl, and you've always been *"Lil' Niki"* to Ric and me. I want to understand what you're doing. Honestly, Nicole, I have never thought of you as a lesbian. Now you've made a commitment, which complicates things a little. I don't want to discourage you or judge you – I just want to understand...Does your mother know?"

"No, she doesn't know. I wanted to be sure before I told her."

"*Are* you sure, Nicole?"

"I have always wanted a partner capable of real friendship, and tenderness, strength and sweet passion. In my somewhat limited experience, I haven't found that in a man. Yet, this relationship with Paula really isn't about a man versus a woman – this is about love. For me it's a choice, *and* a commitment, and I want to make it work," Nicole answered, with conviction.

"Can I ask you how you met and how this relationship started?"

"Well, first of all we're both on the faculty, or rather *were* on the faculty, at the same school. Paula has a reputation as an incredibly talented musician, who is completely devoted to her students. Her department has been winning awards in regional competitions for years. It wasn't like I saw her and decided to seek her out. To be honest, I was ambivalent about even having a friendship with her. I heard she was a lesbian and truthfully, I didn't know how to be around her.

Then, one night I went to the presidential campaign offices to volunteer and there she was –seriously hard at work. I was friendly with her and eventually she invited me to have dinner with her. I wasn't sure what to do, so I made an excuse and put her off a little. When I discussed this with another friend, she asked me '*where I had been for the last fifteen years*'. I had very little experience with the gay community and never gave it much thought. This same friend said to me "*Nicole, really, nobody cares!*' I was feeling kind of ridiculous about it, so I invited Paula to have dinner with me. We talked about the coming elections and the school, just like everyone else was doing at the time. We started going to the movies, concerts, and one night I agreed to go to her house for coffee. Instead of coffee, I had a couple of glasses of wine and for some reason, was feeling kind of attracted to her. We kissed; and by the way, she is a great kisser, and, well, something inside me moved. I don't even know how to describe it…but the truth is – I just said goodnight and went home. I guess I needed some time to think before I got too involved. A week later, she invited me back to her house again. A few more glasses of wine, a kiss, and then well….I felt free and natural and excited and well…."

"Okay, I get the picture…" interrupted Caroline. "But does this mean you don't like men anymore? Come on Nicole, you've also had boyfriends with whom you've had great sex. Can you just switch your sexual orientation? "

"That's a really good question. The truth is, I still find myself attracted to men occasionally, and I don't think I have ever been sexually attracted to women before. Shrinks call it sexual fluidity. Truthfully Caroline, I am very happy just the way things are. I just want to be with Paula; I really do love her. We're a good team. We have the same values and like so many of the same things. We truly have fun together. How often do you find that – male or female?

There is a gay culture out there of very normal happy families, who work, play, raise children and live decent principled lives. Many of them are working hard for simple human rights, so the next generation of gays and lesbians can live with dignity and peace....Of course, it has given me another cause to work for."

"Are you going to have a family?" asked Caroline.

"No, we're not thinking about that. It's too late for us for that. Please promise not to share this with anyone, but Paula recently received a diagnosis that will most likely disable her in another five to seven years...and I want to take care of her, Caroline. In the states that allow gay marriage or registered domestic partners, I can put her on my healthcare insurance. I want to make a commitment to her that will make her feel secure for the rest of her life."

"That's very generous of you honey, and a huge commitment. I'm sorry to hear about her illness, and I promise not to say anything. Do you think she would consider talking to Kate about her condition? Kate is so knowledgeable, and I'm sure she would have something to contribute – if only to delay the inevitable. I'll bet Kate's clinic has a long list of miracles that may be encouraging news for Paula. Please encourage Paula to speak with her. I know she'll do anything she can to help her.

How has Paula's family responded to the news of her illness?" asked Caroline.

"They don't know yet and frankly, I don't think they care. She is one of millions of gay women who have been ostracized by their family, because of, well, just plain ignorance. I will ask her to speak with Kate, though I'm not sure she is willing to share this with anyone just yet."

"That must be very painful, and what about you? What will your mother think?" asked Caroline, sympathetically.

"Come on Caroline...you know exactly what my mother will do. She will refer to Paula as my *'special friend'* and not say another word. Frankly, I don't give a flying fig what other people think! Don't you think we're too old for that?

Do you want to know what really hurts? It's all the times during any given day that you restrain yourself from public displays of affection, so that the rest of the world doesn't feel uncomfortable. It's lousy."

"Well, New Mexico hasn't passed any laws regarding gay marriage yet, but my guess is that it's on the table, just not yet approved," said Caroline.

"No it hasn't, but your governor is trying to get something passed. I'm not sure we will want to live here anyway. I don't see much opportunity for us, and eventually we'll need to live near a good medical facility. But we'll cross that bridge when we get to it," responded Nicole.

"It sounds like I'm asking a lot of basic questions which you clearly have already answered for yourself. I don't mean to pry; I just want you to be happy. It sounds like you are fully committed.

Oh my gosh... I just realized how much I am sounding like Julia!" Caroline said laughingly. "Okay you've told me how you feel about Paula; now tell me what she brings to your life"

"Well, I've already given you purpose, commitment, values and ...let's see...she brings respect, music, laughter and joy to the relationship – things I've not experienced in a very long time. Why do you ask?"

"You don't need to convince me, really... I'm having a relationship with a ghost... I shouldn't be questioning you at all! It sounds like you're doing this for all the right reasons Niki, and if you're happy, then I'm happy. I want to get to know Paula better and make her feel welcome here too."

And with that...both women lay back on the blanket, taking in the warm sun, until they closed their eyes and fell into a sweet summer dream.

Possibilities

"Friendship is born at that moment when one person says to another: 'What! You, too? Thought I was the only one.'"

- C. S. Lewis

*T*he Taos tour proved to be a long day that took its toll on its travelers, and each retreated to her bungalow for a little respite before dinner. JB, feeling a bit repentant, volunteered to be the dinner chef, promising a more gentle dash of spices.

Caroline set the table, which she designed with a southwest theme using colorful glass mosaic votive candles and a Zuni bear fetish at each place setting. The carved bear's smooth texture of turquoise and jasper was enhanced by tiny feather adornments. Caroline chose the bear fetish because it was believed to lighten the weight of emotional burdens, ease difficult decisions, and deepen one's introspective capacities. The bear represented strength in the face of adversity and was the manager of transitions.

Tonight these women were going to discuss their current challenges and try to lovingly support each other through them.

To everyone's pleasure, JB had prepared authentic New Mexico cuisine. Carmen for once, was happy to give up her territorial rights to the kitchen and gladly became a guest rather than the chef. And also tonight, everyone showed a little restraint with the wine. JB's diners enjoyed blue corn enchiladas with a green chili sauce and julienne salads.

"These regional dishes may be commonplace fare for you and Carmen, but in North Carolina, this would be considered gourmet," Diana said to Caroline.

"This would be gourmet cuisine in Sonoma, too." added Kate. "It's simply wonderful!"

"We wouldn't eat this in Chicago," chimed in Nicole and Paula.

"I don't think any of you know this, but the only time that JB cooks at AngelFire is when all of you are here," said Carmen. "He loves your compliments!"

Small bowls of tayberries and bush cherries with a brandy crème sauce were presented for dessert. Carmen stood, raised her glass and gave a toast to her husband, "To JB Robles, a man of many talents and abilities...I am grateful for this delicious meal and for this delicious man." The chef blushed at the praise of his diners.

Amidst the merriment, a cell phone began humming and vibrating in someone's pocket. After a few checks, everyone realized that it was Diana's phone. "I'll leave it for later," she mumbled.

"Have you spoken to him yet?" Caroline asked.

"Once," she answered.

"*Well?*" chorused her seven friends.

"Well, I hung up on him! *Diana, baby, you know I...*" she said imitating Jackson. "Then, I hit the 'end' button."

"Okay Diana baby...how long can you do that?" asked Marti.

"Until I am ready to talk to him."

"Uh-huh, and I'm sure Miss Elaina would be happy to console him in the meantime," said Marti. A gasp echoed across the dining room. "Diana, I have worked in churches all my life and do not know a minister, male or female, that has not been hit on by a congregant. This is not new information for you. The question is *'Is this the first Miss Elaina?'* You need to know if this was a moment or a behavior." Marti's frankness was followed by turned heads and soft murmurs.

"There are other questions, too...like what is my part in this, and have I just been turning my head?" Diana replied.

Caroline chimed in, "I find that hard to believe. However, you can torture yourself with questions or you can confront him... maybe even forgive him, and then create a new marriage with Jackson, on *your* terms. "

"I would like to know all that I have to forgive...before I can move on. Also, I want to feel stronger when I confront him. I feel so vulnerable, so discouraged. My heart is aching," confessed Diana.

"Well, of course your heart is aching, *'cause you love the guy',*" said Carmen. "And that means you still have hope. I would be ready to set new terms for the marriage and for the ministry. Anyway, that's what I had to do with JB."

"JB?" shrieked Siggy and Nicole.

JB dashed into the room...."Did you call me? Is everything ok?"

"Everything is perfect," answered Carmen with a smile. "Thank you." And with that, JB left the room. "See Diana..." she said with a wink. "There is always hope."

"Maybe if I had the heart to forgive Ric, or had been more mature about it, we could have worked things out and wouldn't have divorced," said Caroline. Just the thought of it, silenced her for a brief moment..."But then we wouldn't be here at AngelFire would we?"

"Ric? My brother Ric? Great, now I know I made the right choice," said Nicole.

"What's that supposed to mean?" asked Paula. Nicole did not respond but sunk her head into her hands.

"When was the last time you and Jackson got away by yourselves for a real vacation?" asked Kate. "Maybe neutral grounds

"Okay, okay, you have given me a lot to think about. I would like some time to reflect on your ideas tonight, pray about them, and I'll consider calling him tomorrow," said Diana. She rose from her seat and added, "So my friends, I bid you each adieu, and will return to this conversation in the morning." She walked directly to Caroline and embraced her. "You *were* there, just as you have been so many other times, and now, again." She turned to the others and said, "All of you, I am deeply grateful for your support."

Diana returned to her bungalow with her head spinning and her heart aching.

After Diana's departure, Caroline turned to the others and said, "It's getting late. Why don't we take all our questions up to the top of the mountain tomorrow? I think the Chili Express is still running, or, if not, we'll take the open air ski lifts. We can go up there and clear our heads and maybe get some inspiration or some answers. The scenery is always spectacular, and this time of year, we can hike down through fields of wildflowers. Bring your cameras."

"Sure, I'll go! But tonight I have another date with Robbie Collicci," announced Kate. "I want to go freshen up. So, I guess I'll see you all in the morning."

"Will you be here in the morning?" inquired Marti.

"Yes, I need to know how many for breakfast," added Carmen with a big wide grin. "Will there be two for bungalow number three?"

"*Two for three, if the saints be with me!*" Kate returned in her best Irish brogue. Hoots and hollers, taunts and teases, ran round the room, until Kate blushed.

"Do not mock her," said Marti. "There's not one of us who isn't jealous!"

"I'm not," said Nicole. She took Paula by the hand and said, "Shall we retire?"

"What? We've just been fired!" Paula answered laughingly.

"Fired up – indeed! Good night everyone." Nicole and Paula departed arm in arm.

"Okay then, Siggy, Caroline, anyone want to see a movie?" asked Marti.

"I think I'm ready to go upstairs and call it a night," said Caroline.

"Don't be startin' with that Patsy Cline music again. We know what you're doing up there," teased Marti.

"Well Siggy, it's you and me babe. Let's see what's in her video collection."

"Do you think she has that old video of Lady Chatterley's Lover?" asked Siggy.

Peak Experience

She lit candles

While the steaming water flowed

Lavender sprigs were tossed and swirling

Oils added a subtle perfume

Silently, she slipped deep into the water

The room was clouded in a fragrant mist

No need for music tonight

He was already there

She could feel him

With a gentle kiss upon her neck

He had returned to her

She turned and rose up out of the water

Standing completely still

His spirit was moving toward her

Once again, he merged his *beingness of light* with her

The gift - A moment of pure indescribable bliss

His essence separated from her and turned toward the fog on the mirror

He wrote the words...

I am sorry

And he vanished

Kate & Robbie

"'Stay' is a charming word in a friend's vocabulary."

- Louisa May Alcott

K ate dashed toward her bungalow, eager to prepare for her rendezvous with Robbie. *Tonight, maybe we'll just talk*, she thought. *He will sit by the fire with me, talk and well...* anything more was yet to be determined. She lit the fireplace for ambiance, for she certainly did not need the warmth. Her temperature was rising at the thought of how this night might unfold. So far, conversations with Robbie Collicci had been replete with inquiry. He wanted to know as much about her as she would reveal. Tonight, Kate intended to reverse the course of their discussions and learn more about this man who so intrigued her.

She covered her hair with a scarf and took a quick, hot shower, lathering herself in the essence of white flowers. She breathed deeply and deliberately as she donned a russet tunic and leggings. A light dusting of loose powder and a little shadow on her eyes, and she was ready; yet, she asked herself... *Am I really prepared for what might come this evening?*

Tonight, Kate would ask the questions that were most important to her. She certainly felt the pull of sexual attraction, but was still undecided as to whether she could handle being intimate with a man after denying herself this part of life for so long. Casual sex was never her forte.

With a little trepidation of his own, Robbie knocked at the door, flowers in hand. Kate opened the door and seeing the flowers said, "Robbie, how sweet of you! Thank you!" She invited him in, leading him to the sofa in front of the fireplace.

As she went to find a container for the flowers, Robbie removed his jacket and made himself comfortable. "I don't think I've ever been in this bungalow before. Caroline's interiors always blend in comfort. I think the guests really appreciate her style."

"Yes, she's always lived in lovely, warm and comfortable homes. Even the apartment she shared with Marti in college was terrific. When I think of all the places she's lived, my head spins. I've been in Sonoma for so long I've hardly remember my L.A. days," said Kate. She returned from the kitchen with the flowers squeezed into a water glass. She offered Robbie a glass of wine and returned to the kitchen pouring red for him, and white for herself. Kate asked, "Besides New York, Las Vegas, and AngelFire, where else have you lived?" for an easy start to their conversation.

"I don't really live in AngelFire," he answered. "I have the condo near the resort, but my primary home and business are in Santa Fe. I would only come up here when I would meet with Frank. We would play a little golf, ski, or go fishing – whatever sport the weather provided. I didn't like the trip down the mountain, and as I picked up other clients around here, I decided I should have an office/condo arrangement in AngelFire.

I also lived in Bloomington, Indiana for two years when I was in college. It was like a foreign country to me. The University of Indiana was a top rated university for a degree in business, but the Midwest was too far away from everything I was familiar with. So, I transferred to San Diego State to get my degree, which turned out to be quite the party-school. Unlike my playboy brothers, the party life was just not for me. I was always considered the "geek" of the family, although no one ever said it. Indiana was too far away from the family and San Diego was just far away enough."

"I thought your family was in New York. Did they all move to Las Vegas?" asked Kate.

"No, my mother died when I was eleven. I went to stay with my aunt, Frank's mother, which was supposed to be a temporary situation. Frank's mother and my mother were sisters. My father married again a year later, and I stayed with the family in Las Vegas. I never saw him much after that, and I'm not so sure he was welcome at the Amoroso household. They took me in as their seventh son. Eventually, I called Frank's dad 'Pops' and his mother became my 'Mama', too."

"You're not the seventh son with certain powers are you?" asked Kate, half teasingly.

"Yes and no..." he started.

"Oh my...just what kind of powers do you have?" she interrupted.

Robbie laughed and added, "Sorry, no mythical powers here... I have the power of the checkbook! I've been handling the family finances for decades. Pops used to say, this was "*provvidenza divina*". He thought I was the only person in the family that should handle the estate."

"Why?" she asked.

"Because I came from a place of gratitude, where my four brothers attitudes came from a sense of entitlement, or expectancy and privilege. I love my brothers, so that is all I'll say about that."

"I don't think I ever met any of your other brothers, although I saw them at Frank's funeral. They just sort of came and left," said Kate.

"Yes, and I left with them. They came out of respect, and they left out of respect. I took them back to my house in Santa Fe. They were in shock, just as we all were," said Robbie. He paused and said, "I'd rather talk about my family some other time."

"Okay, then back to your powers Robbie Collicci, seventh son... you certainly seem to have some kind of power over me," she confessed. "This is way out of character for me. I came here to rest, and have fun with my friends, but I find myself more interested in being with you. You've become a powerful distraction from this retreat with my friends. When I arrived, I was exhausted; now, I am feeling rather exuberant. This is not like me, Robbie. Do you always have this effect on women?"

He laughed and said, "What women? I don't date that often Katie. I'm sort of a solitary man. The truth is I am fascinated by you. You live in a world I know nothing about. You have a salubrious freshness about you that invigorates me. It's nice to know that you are getting something in return."

Something in return? That's an understatement, thought Kate. "Would you like another glass of wine?" Kate rose from the sofa, eyes still locked with his...took a deep breath and went into the galley kitchen to retrieve the wine and a small tray of cheese, nuts and chocolate. She turned back, and he was standing there, just inches from her. She set the tray back down on the counter and steadied herself putting one hand on the counter. Robbie took the wine from her other hand and placed it alongside the tray. He put an arm around her waist and drew her to him. His other hand cradled her head, as he tenderly embraced her and ardently kissed her. He breathed deeply as if to inhale the very essence of her. Kate, equally impassioned, melted into him. He was irresistible – this was unstoppable, and in this moment, everything in the world seemed right. For this blissful night, there were no more questions to ask – nothing else to do – but to be with him.

On to the Summit

"Come forth into the light of things; Let Nature be your teacher."

William Wordsworth

J B had the guest van ready for his mountain hikers at ten the next morning. Carmen elected to remain at the office of the Inn, as she had special preparations in mind for the evening's dinner. Seven women in various sizes of jeans, various colors and styles of sweaters, and very interesting ideas about hiking shoes, boarded the AngelFire Inn van. Year after year, JB took these same women up to ride the tram to the top of the ski runs at the AngelFire ski resort, in the Sangre de Christo Mountains. Each time they rode in an atmosphere of joyful anticipation. This year, a slightly more solemn group headed to the mountain. Each woman was seeking answers to her own life's questions, which was drastically different from the rock divas of just two nights before.

Kate noticed Siggy swallowing another aspirin and asked, "Do you have another headache?"

"Just a dull one, really, I'm fine," she answered.

Siggy addressed the whole group, "I stayed up late last night and made a new desert for tonight's dinner. I gave it to Carmen this morning. I really think you're all going to like this one. Yesterday, Katie and Robbie Collicci took me to the grocery store for more supplies."

"Animal, vegetable or mineral?" asked Marti, who received an elbow in the ribs from Caroline.

Ignoring Marti and turning to Kate, Siggy added, "I really like this man, Katie, and he surely seems to think the world of you."

"He's a sweet man," responded Kate. Still concerned she said, "Siggy, please promise you'll let me take a look at you when we return." Siggy nodded silently and looked away.

"Well Katie, do you have anything you would like to share with us this morning? I see a particular glow in your complexion," chided Marti. Six women looked at Kate, waiting for an answer.

"Silence is the golden answer," Caroline said to Kate. "You don't have to tell anything."

"Aw com' on, you're with friends, you can tell us," said Siggy, glad to turn the attention away from herself.

Accustomed to their own clandestine intimacies, Nicole and Paula remained silent.

"Let's just say we fully shared our togetherness," Kate finally divulged, with a glint in her eye.

"You must really care about Robbie," said Diana. "It's not like you to be intimate with a man you've just met. I hope you're able to keep your heart safe."

"I do like him very much. Isn't that just like me to manage to find a good man who lives over thirteen hundred miles away from my home? How safe is *that*?" replied Kate. "I'm trying really hard to just enjoy whatever this is and be open to whatever it could be."

"Well, well, well, ah do declare, awar friend Katie may just be fallin' in luv," said Diana in her best Southern accent. "What evah will she do?"

"She'll be goin' to th' top o' the mountain and offerin' up a wee prayer to St. Valentine – That's what she'll be doin' t'day," Kate responded, in her best Irish brogue.

"I think we all have questions to take to the mountain today," said Nicole. "We should be having a ceremony or something."

"Perhaps the good Reverend Greene would like to lead us in a ceremony?" asked Siggy.

"Perhaps," responded Diana. She was too polite to reject the idea vocally, but Diana had her own pain to deal with and being "*on*" was not exactly what she had in mind.

"We all have decisions to make and we all need answers. I love how the mountain helps put things into perspective for me. I'm glad we're all here at this time together," said Caroline, with a touch of melancholy in her heart. "We need that '*still small voice*'...for a little clarity."

JB drove silently, knowing exactly how Caroline was feeling. He had felt the presence of Frank this morning, too...yet, neither one told the other. He drove onto the ski lodge drive and like any good chauffeur, helped the seven women out of the van. As another gift from the AngelFire Inn, through Carmen's arrangements, he handed each of them lift tickets. Apparently, the Chili Express was offline for the day.

"You take such good care of us," Caroline whispered to this Zuni bear of a man.

"I'll call you in a couple of hours when we're ready to come back to the Inn. I told Carmen we would eat lunch at the Summit Haus. Thank you, JB...for everything."

The women of the AngelFire Inn entered the sturdy ski lodge, eagerly anticipating the spectacular scenery they were about to experience. "No matter how many times I've taken this ride, I am always ecstatic when I see the views up here," said Nicole.

"I never take any of this for granted," said Caroline. "I've been here at least six times since I lost Frank, and no two trips are the same. Carmen has come with me a couple of times, too." Marti put an arm around Caroline's shoulders and gave her a gentle squeeze. No words were necessary.

As they approached the lift corridor, they felt the rush of a chilly mountain wind.

"I've never been on a chairlift before," admitted Paula, with some trepidation.

"Well, you are in for the ride of your life," said Siggy.

The women split into two groups, Caroline, Siggy, Kate and Marti for one chairlift and Diana, Nicole and Paula on the other. Within twenty seconds, they were up and away toward the grand vistas that awaited them.

"Are you okay?" Diana asked Paula after the lift off. "I know it's a little frightening at first, and these open air lifts can be a lot more tenuous than the aerial trams. We won't let you fall, I promise. Which one of you will be taking pictures?"

"I will," said Nicole. "But would you take one of the two of us first? I want one of Paula while her face is frozen with fear. Then we'll take one on the way down, when she realizes that this is heavenly."

Diana took the photo, and as she checked the camera afterward, she leaned over to Paula and said, "You may want to delete this one later."

In the second chairlift, Kate was watching Siggy's breathing patterns as they gained altitude, though she could not help but be distracted by the majestic panorama that lay before her. The splendor of the snowcapped mountains, cradling the lush pristine valley of AngelFire was magnificent. "This is glorious," sighed Kate. "It makes you appreciate everything, doesn't it?"

"I love how it makes my life and all its issues seem so far away. When we're up here and captured by this beauty, I am reminded of what is really important and what is not," added Marti.

"It brings me peace," said Caroline. "Frank and I used to come up here often, too."

"I always wondered why we didn't do this on the first day of our trip here each year," said Siggy. "This year, I think we're doing this on the perfect day. I think we're all standing at crossroads, and maybe today we'll get some divine inspiration on which path to take."

"Crossroads is a good metaphor for each of us, but I'm not clear on your crossroads, Siggy. I'm sorry; I know I haven't been fully present on this retreat, due to my diversions with Robbie," said Kate as she cleared her throat and blushed. "Will you please tell me again what decision you are trying to make?" said Kate.

"Well, I haven't said much because I was hoping this trip would bring new enthusiasm for my latest sweet creations. I have been using my friends as taste testers for about a decade and have burned down a kitchen in the process. Since no one has given any rave reviews about any of my newest creations this week, it may be time to give up 'Siggy's Sweets and Snacks' and move on to something else," she confessed.

"Oh, Siggy, I just tease you a lot, because you take it so well. If this is what you want to do, then don't ever give up. I know how you feel...I've wanted to give up on my music many times and by September I may be performing with the symphony. Hang in there girl, you'll find the right combination," Marti said apologetically.

"Thank you Marti," said Siggy "I guess I'm working on a Sweet Symphony of my own."

"There you go," said Caroline. "Maybe a little sweet you can eat at the symphony! You know, at those little bars and cafés we visit during intermission."

"Okay, healthy snacks for dieters, school children *and* symphony goers. What a week!" she replied with a tone of exasperation.

The chairlift was about to reach a crest on the mountain. They prepared for their landing by holding each other's hand for assistance on the step off onto the mountain. The first group landed smoothly, and they waited close by for the second chairlift. Simultaneous sighs of relief affirmed that no one met with a catastrophe in that most awkward process.

"Does anyone know how to get on and off these things gracefully?" asked Siggy with a frown, as they gathered at the summit.

"Diana does," said Nicole. "No surprise there. *And* she counseled Paula out of her fear, while I took some fabulous pictures!"

"Yes, thank you, Diana," added Paula. "I think Nicole actually enjoyed seeing me so terrified in that thing."

"I did! You, who seem to have the courage of a lion, surprised me! I knew you'd be fine in a few minutes," answered Nicole, while patting her shoulder.

"Okay Caroline, do you have a plan, now that we're here?" asked Marti.

"First we get the annual group photos," she answered. "I wish Carmen were here for this."

They found another hiker who agreed to photograph the company of women. He was kind enough to take several shots from several angles, funny-faced and serious, for the soon-to-be-framed annual retreat photo of the *Women of AngelFire*. Previous photos of these same women donned the halls at the Inn, reflecting the value of their cherished friendships. However, there was nothing serious about these photos. Some were goofy, fun and even outrageous shots. They always posed for at least two shots that were conventional and lovely to look at – so they had at least *one* they could share with their families.

As the photo session concluded, they thanked the photographer and headed toward the descending trail for the long walk down the mountain.

Diana decided to take the lead. "Katie, last night after dinner, you said something that made me take a serious look at myself. You said the first step to getting what you want, is to *know* what you want. It is pointless for me to want what I had in the past. So I have to see *what is real about the present* to decide what I want in the future." She looked around the group and asked, "Am I making any sense?"

"Yes, and that applies to me too," murmured Caroline. *Is Frank's presence real? S*he wondered to herself.

"Me, three," said Marti. "How do I know Erik has an ounce of interest in me or my son? I have just spent the last thirty years denying that this man even existed! I buried the memory of a wonderful summer of love, and locked it away from my reality... until now"

"Uh-me, four" said Katie. "Am I being *real* about Robbie? Am I just out of character and is this some kind of summer fling? I have a clinic that has been my *life!*"

"Well, me five, I guess," said Siggy. "Maybe it is time for me to *'get real'* too."

"Sorry ladies can't join you on this one...I think Paula and I know exactly what we want," said Nicole.

"Well uh, maybe not," said Paula. "I think we need to talk." Nicole blanched.

Caroline stepped to the middle of group to make a suggestion. "Okay, why don't we each walk down the trail until we find a place to sit and meditate, contemplate, reflect or pray, and consider what *is real* to us. Perhaps out of that, we can look forward to what we want. The trail ahead is well marked; you've all done this before. We can meet at the Summit Haus for lunch. Can we meet between noon and twelve-thirty? I want to be back at the Inn early, as there's a strong possibility of rain this afternoon. Let's try not to lose sight of each other."

All agreed and with watches synchronized, the hikers moved silently down the slope. One by one, and the pair, found a rock, a log, or a field of delicate lavender and blue wildflowers. There were silent tears, whispered prayers and vacant stares.

An hour later, Caroline entered the Summit Haus and requested a table for eight. She called Carmen and asked her to steal away to join them for lunch. Carmen arrived twenty minutes later, and Caroline imparted the details of the seven quests for truth. Carmen listened intently then asked, "What about you? Did you have any revelations while you were on the mountain? Do you have any insights you would like to share?"

Caroline hesitated briefly, and then answered, "I want to talk about this at home, when we're alone. Here comes Diana and it looks like Paula and Nicole are following closely. They rode the chairlift together, and they may have an unfinished conversation in progress. It seems there may be a change of plans in the works for Paula and Nicole." She had avoided answering Carmen, yet again. All three women arrived nearly breathless. They seated themselves and lifted their water glasses before speaking.

"I don't think I have ever been anywhere this beautiful in my whole life," said Paula as she pulled up her chair. "I mean it, Caroline; I know exactly why you continue to live up here in these mountains. It does seem rather isolated, but I think that is trivial compared to the magnificence of the mountains. The Taos trip was altogether interesting too, and as the newbie of this group, I feel incredibly grateful for your hospitality. I am invigorated by the beauty that surrounds me and the beauty in each of you." Paula was glowing, and it was the most talkative she had been since she arrived.

"Thank you Paula, that was lovely," responded Caroline. "I'll never forget my first trip to AngelFire. Frank and I came up from the south. We were driving through the forest, and we had to stop the car when a herd of antelope crossed the road. I had never seen antelope in the wild before – only in the zoo! I burst into tears. I'm not sure exactly why, but they were just so beautiful."

At that moment, Marti sauntered in with a smile on her face. "Good afternoon ladies, I trust you've each come down from the mountain a little wiser? I think I did, and I know what I am supposed to do next. Now all I have to do is muster up the courage to do it." Her friends responded with a round of good wishes.

"Carmen, I'm so glad you could join us," said Diana. "This has been an important day for each of us. At least I hope so. There is nothing like our mountain cathedral for inspiration."

"Let's order," said Nicole. "This mountain also stimulates my appetite! I'm sure Kate and Siggy are right behind us...uh...what's with the helicopters? Are they searching for someone?"

"I saw Buck Whitley on the way in, and he told me the Sky Team was training a new pilot today. They're practicing some search and rescue maneuvers before the snow sets in," answered Carmen.

"The noise was quite a distraction from our deliberations. It kind of steals the peace," commented Paula.

"What noise?" asked Diana.

Orders were taken and drinks delivered. By now, Carmen was getting concerned about the two women who had not yet joined them. "Do you think that Kate and Siggy got lost?"

"I hope not," answered Caroline. "They shouldn't have...we all know this trail and it is well marked."

"I think I see Kate coming now. Siggy is probably with her," reported Marti.

Kate approached the table and said, "Sorry, I took so long. I was in a deep meditation up there and lost track of time." She scanned the table and noticed the empty chair. "Isn't Siggy with you?"

"We thought she was with you!" said all five, now worried women.

"I'll go back and look for her," said Caroline. "Carmen do you have your phone? Katie, please come with me, just in case...the rest of you enjoy your lunch. Order something for Kate and Siggy, please. I'm sure we'll find her in a few minutes and join you."

"She's probably picking a state flower, illegally, and those helicopters are probably a New Mexico swat team landing to arrest her," Marti jibed.

"I think I'd almost believe that," said Nicole.

The luncheon arrived and all five ravenous women began to eat – with expectations that the remaining three would join them within minutes. Talk of the ride up, the views, and comparisons to previous years trips to the mountain ensued.

Caroline and Kate quickly retraced the trail, scanning the surrounding areas for Siggy, expecting her to be perched on a rock or more likely lost in a conversation with other hikers along the way and exchanging recipes. Halfway up the trail, Kate caught a glimpse of Siggy's bright red sweater, in a field of flowers. "Caroline! Over here!" Kate shouted, breaking into a run. Caroline quickly dashed up beside her.

They found Siggy, slumped over, face down, and unconscious, her right hand holding a bouquet.

Kate knelt down beside her, and felt her pulse. "Siggy, can you hear me?" she asked gently, and repeatedly.

"Oh God, tell me she's sleeping," pleaded Caroline. They turned Siggy over, and found that her head was bleeding from a gash on her forehead.

"Do you have your phone?" asked Kate. "Call Carmen and get some help."

Caroline called Carmen, and in minutes a helicopter landed in the field about twenty-five feet away. A paramedic jumped out and pushed Kate out of the way. Within seconds, Siggy was awake.

"What happened? Can you tell us what happened?" Though he had to shout over the noise of the helicopter, he asked calmly and efficiently.

"I don't know," she stammered. "I was picking flowers, then... well, I don't remember."

"You're going to need a few stitches on your forehead. It looks like you hit this rock when you fell. Your blood pressure is pretty high right now," he said. "We're going to take you over to the hospital in Taos to have them take a look at you, just to be safe, so just relax."

"I'll go with you," shouted Kate. She turned to Caroline and whispered, "She's going to be fine. She needs first aid – not a hospital. I'll call you later. Go ahead and get back to the others."

"Are you sure?" Caroline asked. "Is she going to be all right?"

"If you had a helicopter buzzing about thirty feet away from your bleeding head and were about to be airlifted to a hospital, your blood pressure would be up too," assured Kate.

"I'll send someone for you," Caroline shouted as she watched her friend be carried on a stretcher and loaded into the helicopter. The thundering, pounding and blasting winds from the helicopter descended deep into Caroline's bones. She shivered as she watched it fly in ominous skies toward Taos. She dreaded that there might actually be something seriously wrong with Siggy, yet she was comforted by the fact that Kate was with her, *woo-woo and all.*

New Beginnings and the End

"The bird a nest... the spider a web... the human a friendship."

- William Blake

our of the seven women retreated to their bungalows for rest and reflection on their trip to the mountain. Kate and Caroline communicated by cell phone during each phase of Siggy's care at the hospital. JB was on his way to Taos to rescue and return them to AngelFire. The coming rains portended a perilous return to AngelFire, as the twenty-five mile journey to Taos was a series of blind curves on a mountain road.

Since tonight's dinner called for comfort food, Carmen had prepared a pot of Green Chile Chicken Stew, a popular basic dish in New Mexico. Salads and homemade tortillas would complete the meal, except for the dessert, which was Siggy's creation. Carmen insisted on setting the table herself. She placed eight small wildflower bouquets in bud vases around the table. A large tureen became the centerpiece, and individual bird totems were positioned at the top of each place setting. Folded place cards for each of her seven diners, including Kate and Siggy, were placed next to the birds. The outside of the card was printed with the guest's name, while the inside noted the symbolism of the bird. Carmen placed herself at the head of the table. This was her night, to share her talents and gifts with the seven women.

At six-thirty, JB, Siggy and Kate still had not arrived. Carmen lit the candles and summoned the others to the dining room. It appeared that the forecasters were correct and a summer night's storm was threatening.

Caroline entered the room with a sling of extra logs for the fire she had lit an hour earlier. "It will be chilly tonight," she said as she iced the wine; and one by one, the others entered the dining room. The first comments were regarding the aroma of the stew and were followed by compliments on the ambience and the unique beauty of the table.

"Carmen this is wonderful. Every year you surprise us with your talent and ingenuity," said Nicole. You know, when I think about regional foods in this country, New Mexico fare even beats Chicago pizza for me. I think I could learn a lot from you."

"What's the latest on Siggy and Kate? Can I assume they are on their way here?" asked Marti. "Should we just have a glass of wine and then wait for them?"

"The last I heard, Siggy's forehead had been stitched up and, of course, she was in good spirits. They are waiting for the doctor to release her. JB is on his way to Taos to get them. We frequently lose cellular service on that mountain trip, so I hope they call as they leave the hospital," reported Caroline, sounding uneasy.

"My husband has driven that road a thousand times, and you can be sure they will be safe," assured Carmen.

"It's a two thousand foot ascent up a mountain ridge, and I'm glad you were the one driving yesterday, Carmen. Even though we make the trip up from Taos every year, I still don't like that drive," said Diana.

Caroline poured the wine. Although she tried not to show her concern, it was written all over her face. She hated these thunder and lightning storms, regardless of how normal they were for the region.

"This wine is wonderful. Who selects the wines each night?" asked Paula.

"Je suis L'Sommelier," answered Caroline, trying to lighten up. "I visit a winery or two each time I go to see Kate in Sonoma. I have learned a lot, yet really it's just about what tastes good to me. Frank and I often went to the wineries here in New Mexico, too. When we found something we liked, he made some kind of business arrangement with them, and now they're delivered here weekly. He knew much more about wine than I do."

When all agreed that it was time for a second glass of wine, Carmen announced, "Let's get started. I can heat up more stew for them when they arrive. They could be another hour."

Each found her place card and took her seat. Diana led with a prayer for the value of good friends, a perfect healing for Siggy and safe travel on the mountain. "Amens" were followed by praise for the savory stew. The salad, tossed with apricots, pine nuts, and fresh tarragon, with pomegranate vinaigrette was a wonderful complement.

"So how was Patsy this evening?" teased Marti. "I heard her singing up there."

Caroline glared at her and said, "It was nothing, only a few minutes...nothing at all."

"Where did you find these beautiful birds Carmen?" interrupted Diana.

"I bought them when we went to Taos, in one of the galleries," Carmen said proudly. "After we eat dinner, I'll tell you what each of them represents."

"How thoughtful, Carmen," said Diana. "You truly are a gem."

"Yes, it's true. I don't know how we would run this place without you, especially this year," added Caroline.

Carmen blushed and said, "I came in to this group over ten years ago, as Caroline's friend. You had known each other for most of your adult lives and were like a family, yet you took me into this beautiful circle of friends without hesitation. I don't have the same history with you, but I get just as excited as Caroline when the planning begins for these annual retreats.

This year I wanted to give you something besides good food. So please sit right where you are. Your plates will be cleared, and I will share with you the story of your totems."

When they finished eating, two servers appeared from nowhere, cleared the plates, swept crumbs from the table linens, and poured another glass of wine for everyone.

"Leave those two extra place settings," directed Carmen. "They will be joining us within the hour." She turned to the others and said, "Maybe Siggy will be here in time to present her dessert."

"Carmen, tell us please, is it something that is very tiny and very light? I couldn't eat another bite," said Paula.

"I am telling nothing." she answered with a smile. Carmen instructed her helpers to place the desert platter on the buffet in the butler's pantry. She urged them to clean up quickly as it was beginning to rain, and she wanted them to get home safely.

"Why do I have two birds?" asked Caroline.

"I'll explain later as we go around the table." Carmen took a deep breath and began her presentation. "First, I'd like to start with Paula and Nicole. Paula, I want to personally welcome you to this group of fine women. You came into this circle like I did, as a friend to one of this family of women. I hope you feel as comfortable with us as we feel with you. I've seen how the two of you interact and noticed how tender you are with each other. Both of you are loved and loving, desired and desiring, adored and adoring. You both are a free expression of woman love. I have placed before you a pair of geese. We know they are birds of migration, and that they are gifted navigators. When one is injured, the other will stay with its fallen comrade. These geese are symbols of fellowship, determination, teamwork, bravery and loyalty. I hope you have migrated here to New Mexico and will be staying for good."

Tears welled up in their eyes, as Nicole nodded to Paula, to speak first. "Carmen, you speak from your heart. I am overwhelmed by how everyone here has welcomed me. I thank you from the bottom of my heart."

Nicole cleared her throat, then added "Carmen, you've touched on all the reasons why this partnership will indeed work. I do want to share with everyone that Paula and I had a meaningful conversation on the mountain today, and we have made some decisions. I'd like to announce, with Paula's permission, that we *are* going to look for jobs here in New Mexico. We agreed that the commitment we have to each other is perfectly fine as it is...and also, I will stop speaking for Paula, as I have been all week."

"That's wonderful Nicole! Welcome to New Mexico!" said Caroline. "Paula, I'm so happy for you both." Applause and cheers followed.

When the peacceful ambiance resumed, Carmen turned toward Marti; however, suddenly the roar of nearby thunder interrupted her.

Caroline checked her cell phone for a return message from Kate. She quickly dialed the number again, but it went straight to Kate's voicemail. She sighed, nervously. Carmen placed her hand on Caroline's and said "It's okay, JB is with them. You know how cell service is out there in this weather. He makes that drive in the dead of winter. They'll be fine; trust him."

Caroline grimaced and mumbled an apology.

Carmen turned back toward Marti and said, "Marti, you have always brought joy to this company of women through your humor. Now that you have revealed the truth about Erik's father, I see you as a whole and complete woman, who has cloaked the life force of an undying love for one man, your entire adult life. You denied any other man's love and completely dedicated yourself to the protection of your son. You display the feminine aspects of courage, pliancy and responsiveness. I gave you the Sparrow, because the sparrow is inclusive and friendly, and it is a symbol of protection. It is also a symbol of creativity, which applies to your music, where I think you have also channeled your love. You've protected your heart and your son, and now I hope you let your heart help you decide what you are going to do next."

"*His eye is on the sparrow,*" sang Diana.

"Thank you Carmen, you flatter me. What you have seen as courage, I have nearly always seen as fear. I have denied Erik's father, misled my son, and have lived with the abandonment of my family. I would much rather see myself through your eyes. I, too, made a decision on the mountain. I have to write to Erik tomorrow and tell him about his son. When I see what his reaction is, I will decide how I am going to tell the truth to my son.

My composition for the music academy this year is called Erik's Theme. Everyone will think that it's for my son; and in a way it is, for he is the outcome of my story, but the truth is ...I wrote it for both of them. By the way, if it is accepted...you are all invited to the concert."

Caroline rose and lifted her glass as a toast to Marti for her courage. Words of encouragement for her musical endeavors and for taking the step toward truth, followed. Caroline had been through every chapter of Marti's story, and now Marti was finally ready to take the most fearful step of all. "I'll help you in any way I can," Caroline whispered.

The night skies were rumbling and the storm was rapidly approaching. Thunderclouds began to conceal the moonlight, creating exceptional darkness. Caroline threw another log on the fire.

Carmen turned to her left and spoke to Diana. "It is no stretch to see you as the swan, my friend. Your elegance and grace are the essence of femininity. You are beauty, and devotion, strength and wisdom. The swan is a symbol of the glory of nature and the power of love. Swans are most often partnered for life. I know you are struggling right now over Jackson. My prayer is that this marriage is not irreparably damaged."

"I am grateful for your sincerity, Carmen. I have a confession and a resolution. I sat on that mountain today and cried like a baby, like I have done every night this week. I realized how dependent I am on Jackson, for who I am. No woman should lose her identity in a marriage, no matter how many years they have been together. Unfortunately, that is a difficult task for most women. I've been with Jackson since I was a sophomore in college. Our lives are so interwoven that I think it would have been impossible for him to have another life which I didn't know about. Perhaps it was divine intervention that led me to walk into that choir room at the moment when I did.

This afternoon, I called him. He will be on a plane tomorrow morning, and tomorrow afternoon he is going to the mountain with me. We will find a place up there and work this out. I have decided that I no longer want to be in the background. I, as a woman, have something to say *and* I can say it on TV, too. I will become all that I am and all I am meant to be."

"Amen," said Marti.

Women rose, glasses clinked and an enthusiastic response followed. A loud crack of thunder and lightning jolted them out of their reverie. Carmen downplayed the interruption by offering tea or coffee to the diners who were still waiting for their missing friends. "You probably guessed that the hummingbird would be for Kate, sweet, hard-working Kate. And only one bird in our circle would wear a bright red coat, all year long, that would be Siggy! She is the Cardinal – Our passionate, warm and spunky bird! We'll hear their mountain revelations when they return. Maybe Kate and Siggy have made decisions they will share with us, too. They should be here in another half hour or so. Who would like some dessert?" She tried to distract Caroline and the others from worrying about the storm. It was dark and eerie and all too familiar.

"All right, let's get into it before Siggy returns, so we can figure out what we'll say to her," said Marti.

"She may want to go straight to bed. It's been a harrowing day for her," added Carmen, "And I don't think we should keep this until tomorrow." Carmen went to the butler's pantry for the large tray. "She put a lot of time into this one ladies," said Carmen as she placed two linen napkins over the top to enhance the presentation. She proceeded into the dining room, placing the tray in the middle of the table, and announced, "Ladies, I present to you Siggy's Symphony Sweets!" She whipped the napkins off of the tray and all six women gasped with delight. A beautiful tray of tiny little pies lay before them. Carmen proclaimed, "Siggy calls them "Two-Bite Pies". There is pumpkin, cherry, pecan, boysen-berry and apple."

"Just like Thanksgiving!" said Nicole. "I'll be happy to take one of each!"

"This is certainly one of the most beautiful desserts she's ever made. She's put her artistic touch on each one of them." said Marti. "I'd like to try the pecan, please and um...the blueberry." Marti took a bite of the petite pecan pie, then said, "And might I add, *Yum*?"

"And with only two bites, one doesn't need to feel guilty!" added Paula. "She may just have something here. I'll try the pumpkin."

"They are healthy, too," said Carmen. "There's no sugar in them. She said she used a calorie-free stevia product."

"I would buy these and keep them in my freezer anytime," said Diana. "They make a beautiful presentation, and this cherry pie is scrumptious!"

"Finally, I think she's found it! I wish she were here right now, I'd love to congratulate her!" said Caroline. Glasses clinked again – this time they had switched to water glasses – "*A toast to Siggy*!"

The weather intensified, threatening a violent storm. Car-men noticed the worrisome expressions on Caroline's face, and decided to take the plunge and finish her presentation.

Paula had slipped away for a quick trip to the restroom, and as she returned, she stopped to view the framed photos on the din-ing room walls before returning to her chair. As she sat down, she commented, "These are beautiful photos of the four of you. Your husband was a handsome man, Caroline."

"Yes, he was," responded Caroline.

"What happened to the huge pine tree in front of the Inn?" she asked.

"Not now," Nicole whispered, extending her hand to Paula.

Carmen quickly turned to Caroline and said, "I want to finish with your birds now. The first one is the Eagle, and this eagle represents Frank. He was our male guardian, nourishing everything in us that was already strong. He was the dominant force for AngelFire. The eagle also symbolizes freedom. Caroline, Frank needs to be free to move on to what is next for him. We cannot hold him back. You cannot keep him here." The room became silent, apart from clatter of the rain on the dining room windows. Tears welled and streamed down Caroline's face. She said nothing. The aching lump in her throat kept her from responding.

"The second bird is the Robin. It is welcomed each year as it joins Mother Earth who blesses us with the season of spring. It symbolizes renewal, rejuvenation, and new beginnings. Caroline you are Life, expressing as an amazing woman, who like your husband, is free. He is meant to be in the great mystery, and you still have more to do here. In your pain you have refused to look forward. Your family, friends and I want to help you do that. We will help you find something to look forward to, whatever that may be."

Caroline covered her face for a moment, as the others quietly watched. She then cleared her throat and responded. "You have each made important decisions up on the mountain today, and I am happy for you. Until this moment, I was going to announce that I too had made a decision. My decision was not to change anything, to stay content right where I am, with Frank, just as he is right now. I was willing to stay in the winter of my grief. Then, I went upstairs this afternoon, and I called out to him. He didn't respond, and I couldn't feel his presence. As you spoke to me I realized he could be here only to give this message that Katie has talked about, and then vanish again from my life.

And Marti, I have been nudging you for years to stop holding your heart closed, thinking that you and Erik may have another chance, another time. I could let the Inn swallow me up, like Katie has said about her clinic, and wonder where my life went. And Diana, I have lost myself in my love for Frank as you have for Jackson. I still love him, but I guess I have to figure out who I am without him. Unlike you, my husband is gone, and I don't know what else I want." She could no longer hold back her tears.

As Carmen and Diana tried to comfort her, Marti declared, "They're here! I see lights coming up the drive."

Caroline broke away and went toward the front entrance. She flung open the door and ran into the storm to greet them. The rain would disguise her tears. The thunder broke into a rolling roar and the wind was screaming through the trees. Carmen and Marti chased after her. Diana and the others followed closely behind.

JB stopped the van and helped Kate get out. He headed straight for Carmen. She embraced him and cried, "I'm so glad you're here. Even I was beginning to get worried."

"It was a rough ride...there was a terrible accident ahead of us, and it took almost an hour to get around it," he answered, still holding her.

"Katie! Are you okay?" Caroline asked, shouting at her, as the storm was now in full force. "Where's Siggy?"

"They want to do an MRI in the morning, to figure out why she's fainting," Kate answered returning the shout. "I tried to call you from the van, and then my phone battery died!"

"Caroline, look!" said JB, pointing in toward the Inn.

Standing in front of the Inn, about thirty feet away, stood a specter of light, in the outline of a man. It was pulsating, and glowing, as...it watched them.

Caroline turned and walked directly, without hesitation, toward what she knew was in essence, Frank. Tonight he would show himself to all of them. Kate was one step behind Caroline. The others were a few feet behind. She stood in front of the gathering and looked at him intently. Lightning crashed in the sky and some of the women screamed. But for Caroline, the world had stopped. She heard nothing. He was there and she could see the shadowed features of his face. "It is you...isn't it, Frank. Have you come back for me?" she asked softly so the others couldn't hear. She could not perceive his answer. Within seconds, he was looking more like an apparition, and she could more clearly detect his features. She could look into his eyes.

"No, Caroline, he hasn't come back for you," said Kate, now standing about four feet behind her. "It's not what you think."

Caroline remained still, eyes locked with his. Carmen stepped closer and asked, "What do you want Frank? How can we help you?"

"He doesn't need your help," yelled Katie.

"Frank?" asked JB, and the women parted to let him through. He stepped forward and stood next to Caroline. He was dazed and visibly shaken. "We tried, we tried so hard…" he said with his voice cracking. "I'm sorry,…so sorry."

The image shook his head as if to say *"No"*. Frank raised his hand to JB's shoulder.

"He knows that," interpreted Kate. "He doesn't want you to feel guilty."

JB embraced his wife and sobbed, then turned back toward Frank, trying to understand the vision that stood before him. Carmen did her best to console her husband.

"What exactly happened here?" Paula asked Marti. They were standing out of hearing distance from the others. Marti took Diana's arm, indicating Diana answer for her, as she was deeply moved and unable to talk. Diana shouted back, "There was a horrible storm, just like this one. Two horses had bolted and gotten loose. JB and Frank were out here trying to get them back into the barn. As they were coming back toward the house, lightning struck the huge pine tree that used to be right where Frank is standing, now. It split and fell on Frank. JB tried everything to lift it off of him. Caroline and Carmen had been watching from a window, and when they saw the lightning hit the tree, they ran out to see that their husbands were all right. Frank was pinned under the tree, and JB was trying to lift it off of him. All three of them tried to move the tree to save Frank, but they couldn't lift it. Frank died right there, in the spot where he is standing now."

Lightning struck again, so close to them that it evoked screams from all but Caroline. Carmen pulled JB a step backwards. The rain was hammering the ground.

"What is it Frank?" Caroline asked softly, as if she and he were removed from the scene completely. There was a glowing light around both of them now. Frank raised his hand and touched her face. "Why did you write *'I'm Sorry'* on the mirror?" He then pointed toward Kate. "What does Kate have to do with this?" she asked without turning toward Kate.

"I don't think it's me," said Kate. "Ask him if it's Robbie," she shouted.

"Does Robbie have something to do with this Frank?" He nodded slightly. Carmen looked up at JB, but he was fixated on the image of Frank. Caroline was completely mesmerized. "Will he know what this is about Frank? I don't understand."

Frank's essence began to pulsate and became less intense. Caroline screamed breathlessly, "Don't leave me Frank, *don't* leave!" She stepped forward.

Carmen reached for her arm and cried "Stop! Caroline! Stop!"

Caroline stepped *right into him and was absorbed by him.* For an instant, she disappeared. Seven screams rang into the rain. Thunder and blinding lightning struck again so closely that everyone instinctively covered their eyes and heads.

In another instant, Frank had disappeared and Caroline was on the ground, on her knees, sobbing. A guttural roar erupted from deep within her. The residue of grief and mourning stored in her body was bursting forth and being released.

JB knelt to console her, yet his own grief was pouring out and stirring into hers. Carmen wrapped herself around both of them. Rain pounded their backs as each woman gathered in the huddle of mourners.

They remained together in the fierce storm until they could wail no more.

Revelations

"Are you upset little friend? Have you been lying awake worrying? Well, don't worry...I'm here. The flood waters will recede, the famine will end, the sun will shine tomorrow, and I will always be here to take care of you."

-Charlie Brown to Snoopy

*T*he stillness before dawn offered little solace for Caroline. The storm had passed and each of her friends had returned to her bungalow, to weep alone. Caroline was curled upon the window seat, draped in an afghan that Julia had made for her. She gazed at the grand lawns of AngelFire for the remainder of the night trying to grasp what had happened. The birds had not yet welcomed the sun with their morning songs. The rain soaked landscape left puddles scattered on the long driveway that lead to the Inn. It was four o'clock; *"the hour of the Angels"*, as Julia used to say. Everything was still, except her mind. Her body was limp, and drained of any emotional or physical strength.

She had only one thing to do today. In four hours, she would call Robbie Collicci.

JB and Carmen stayed the night at their house, on the Angel-Fire property. Mentally, physically and emotionally exhausted, they held each other until they fell asleep.

Marti, Diana, Nicole and Paula had trudged back to their bungalows, one by one, each without an awareness of the other. Everyone needed to interpret for themselves what they had witnessed.

At eight, with justified apprehension, Caroline made the call. Robbie seemed prepared to hear from her; she was too numb to care. She dressed in jeans and a white shirt and pulled her hair back with a headband, as that was all she could manage. No makeup; no jewelry. When she descended the stairs to the kitchen, she noticed the aroma of coffee that had already been made. A note from Carmen was sitting on the counter.

Received a call - storm damage at the high school - We love you, C & JB

Caroline tossed it aside and poured herself a cup of coffee, thinking it would at least help her be a more alert driver. She pulled her Volvo out of the garage and slowly maneuvered it off the property as quietly as possible. She drove into town knowing that a mystery was about to be solved, and Robbie Collicci held the key.

Robbie had been waiting for her. At long last, he would tell her everything. He told her he had given his assistant the day off, and his telephones would be set for voicemail. They would take as much time as she needed. He offered her more coffee, and she took it.

Caroline spoke first, "Robbie, first I want to say I am sorry for taking so long to come to see you. I'm sure you've been paying the bills all year, wondering if I thought there was some kind of bottomless well for a bank account. I know we haven't had the same number of guests as we usually do but..."

"Stop, Caroline," Robbie interrupted. "Apologies are not necessary. In fact, it is I who should be apologizing," confessed Robbie.

"Why?" asked Caroline.

"Because, I should have told you what you had to work with, right away. I should have been sending you statements. I shouldn't have been in collusion with Frank though all of this. You had a right to know years ago. I think Frank was so happy with you and your life together at the Inn, that he just didn't want anything to change. Frank had the ability to create his own little world his whole life," said Robbie.

"What do you mean his whole life? How would you know that Robbie?" she asked.

"He never told you, did he? Frank and I are...or were, cousins, and we grew up together, like brothers. I have handled the Amoroso family money since college, until he and I moved here to New Mexico. We sort of split with the family and came here to start something new, something clean, you know...a fresh start," he admitted.

"Do I really want to know this?" Caroline asked, with her head buried in her hands. "Am I really ready to hear what secrets my husband kept from me? Robbie, I don't know if I have the strength to hear all the facts this morning. I came here because I want to know where I stand. I also want to help out some friends of mine. I want to go back to the Inn and give them some good news," she declared.

"I'm sure you have enough to help as many friends as you want. Let me get your last financial statement. Your books are up to date. I just held these statements until you and I had a chance to sit down and go over everything. I don't know if you were aware of Franks other business."

"His what?" Caroline gasped.

"Okay, Caroline....I guess we do have a lot to talk about," Robbie said nervously. He pulled one of several large green ledger books from a shelf behind his desk. He opened it and placed it in front of Caroline. "First, here is your total net worth. I'll break it down in a minute."

Caroline ran her index finger down the page as she looked at the accounts. Some she recognized, and others she did not. When she reached the bottom of the page, she blanched and her hand began to shake.

"Caroline?" said Robbie, as he quickly handed her a glass of water. "Are you okay? You look as if you're about to faint."

"Where did this come from?" she asked incredulously.

For the next hour and a half, Robbie revealed the truth of Frank's past and his hidden finances. Caroline's first response was disbelief. They argued and shouted. She cried and seemed unconvinced. Why would he do this? Were we living a lie? By the end of the meeting, Caroline was beyond exhaustion. She shared with him her intentions and made Robbie swear to continue this secrecy until she decided what to do next.

Caroline drove back to the Inn, her mind reeling with new questions. Is this what Frank was trying to tell her? Was he trying to apologize from the other side? Why did he feel the need for all his secrets to begin with?

Arriving at the Inn, she returned the car to the garage, as quietly as she'd taken it. Unaware of any one moving about the property, she moved stealthy to the rear entrance and went directly to the staircase. She was in a near stupor as she climbed the stairs to her apartment, landed on her bed, and finally succumbed to the exhaustion of the past twenty-four hours.

Sorting What's Real

"I awoke this morning with devout thanksgiving for my friends, the old and the new."

- Ralph Waldo Emerson

Marti thought she was the first one to face the morning when she entered the Inn and found it silent. She went directly to the kitchen, and found the note from Carmen and JB near the coffee pot. After pouring a cup of coffee, she sat in the breakfast nook, waiting for Caroline to come down the stairs. She stared out of the window, still mulling over the events of the night before. A noise came from the entry. It was Paula and Nicole, looking equally bleary eyed, still in their robes, and in desperate need of coffee.

"We're out of coffee in our place. Is everyone else still sleeping?" whispered Nicole.

"JB & Carmen are at the high school in Taos. I guess the storm did some damage. They left a note," answered Marti. "Caroline must still be asleep." Marti went to the counter and poured two

more cups of coffee, and Nicole and Paula joined her in the circular booth.

Nicole yawned and said, "I feel like I am trying to wake up from some kind of bizarre dream."

"Is it possible that we all dreamed the same dream last night?" asked Paula. She stretched her arms above her head and exhaled, then took another sip of her coffee and said, "Whatever that was we saw last night, it spoke to how powerful their relationship was, or still is, I guess. I'll be interested to hear what Kate and Diana thought about last night."

"Speaking of Madame Zara..." teased Marti, as Kate entered the room.

Kate, unlike her friends, was not bleary eyed and even looked rested. She greeted them and went directly to the refrigerator where she found some juice and mixed a blend of powders into it. Kate stirred it briskly as she walked to the table and said to Marti, "Scoot over unbeliever."

Marti slid over and made room for Kate. She could not let up on her friend and on behalf of everyone, posed the question, "Would you like to enlighten those us who do not have your powers, Madame? When did you turn into *a ghost whisperer*?"

Kate took a long drink of her herbal concoction and ignored Marti.

"*Therefore, she doth not speak*," said Nicole. "Whatever it was that you were doing last night, it seemed accurate and I'm impressed."

Marti asked, "Really Kate, how often *do* you do this?"

"Well," started Kate..."How often have you ever witnessed anything like that?"

"Never," answered the two teachers simultaneously.

"Are you saying you never did this before?" asked Marti.

Kate took a deep breath, but before she could respond, they were interrupted by a noise from the entry. Diana was trying to be as quiet as possible, but the squeaky hinges on the entry door announced her arrival.

"I thought I was the first one up," said Diana. She too, looked rested, was fully dressed, and in a surprisingly cheerful mood. "Kate, I don't know what you gave me last night, but I think I slept on the moon."

"You probably haven't had a good night's sleep since you got here," replied Kate. "I just gave you a little something to help you relax."

"Excuse me?" exclaimed Marti, just above a whisper. "You didn't think the rest of us would have a little trouble sleeping last night, after witnessing a demonstration of the 5th dimension?"

Diana intervened, "I went to Kate because I remembered that she gave Julia something at the funeral last year, which pretty much knocked her out. With Jackson coming today, I needed to be rested and strong. He'll be here in a few hours."

"Well, now that the witnesses have gathered, what do we think about what happened last night?" asked Nicole.

"Before you speak, has anyone checked on Caroline?" asked Diana.

"Not a sound from her room, and Carmen and JB are in Taos," answered Marti.

"I'm not sure what I saw, but I do know how I felt," said Nicole. "Caroline was in agony, and my whole body wanted to cry with her."

"Grief is a powerful emotion. It can make a person so fragile they can't be rational, or it can make them stronger. I don't think it has anything to do with how much you love the person you've lost. I think it has to do with how much you defined yourself through your relationship with that person....then again, every-one is different," counseled Diana.

"I think that last night proved that none of us really know any-thing and that anything is possible!" said Kate.

"And I've counseled many women who would love to call their husbands back from the other side," Diana added.

The discussion continued for half an hour. Coming to an agreement on what they saw, *or didn't see,* was a more difficult task than they'd expected.

"I know there are several theories about this, but maybe it's not our business to know," said Marti.

"I've learned in my business that just when you think you've seen it all, something else shows up," said Kate with conviction. "You may be right; maybe we just don't need to know. By the way, I called Robbie and asked him to take me back to the hospital to get Siggy this morning. I called her, and the nurse said she was getting the MRI, and if all was well, she'd be released by noon. Robbie's phone must have been turned off because it went straight to voicemail."

"Maybe Carmen and JB can bring her back with them," Marti suggested.

"No, I'd rather be there when she gets the initial report. I want to see where the neurologist is going with this. I know she doesn't have a brain tumor or anything else serious, and I'd rather work with them than against them," added Kate.

"So what do we want to do today, Ladies? Diana has to deal with Jackson. Katie asked Robbie to take her to Taos. Ladies? Do you have any other ideas?" asked Marti.

"You have a letter to write, don't you?" asked Kate. "No more avoidance Marti, okay?"

"I think I'll go on the Internet and do some job searching," said Nicole.

"Kate, I'd like to spend a little time with you before you go to the hospital. If I may impose, I'd like to discuss something personal with you," said Paula, rather sheepishly.

"Of course, let's walk back to my bungalow. I left my cell phone in there, and I don't want to miss Robbie's call."

"We also need to plan a surprise for Siggy. That dessert was her best yet! So let's see how she is feeling and plan to do something special for her at dinner. Maybe we should all go out to dinner tonight. We could include Jackson, Robbie and JB, if all goes well," suggested Marti. "Are we all in agreement?"

"I think that is a wonderful idea, and I think rest is in order today," said Kate.

"Yes, Dr. Kate," said Nicole.

"Thank you, Dr. Woo-Woo," added Marti.

"One more thing," Diana began. "About last night, how about if we all agree that we just saw Caroline say goodbye to her husband. That's it and it stays here; it doesn't leave AngelFire."

As the women were about to respond in accordance, they heard the back door open. Caroline hurried through the door and walked straight through the kitchen, oblivious to those in the room. She climbed the stairs and went directly to her apartment and closed the door behind her.

All witnesses sat open-mouthed and remained silent.

Revelation Revealed

"My friends are my estate."

- Emily Dickinson

At five o'clock that evening, Caroline had showered, dressed and was prepared to face her friends. She went down to the kitchen and found Carmen and JB at the table. Both rose to meet her. "Are you ready to do another dinner party tonight, or would you rather be left alone?"

"I am as alone as I would ever want to be," she replied. "But before everyone arrives, I want to talk to both of you." Caroline joined them at the table.

Carmen poured a cup of tea for Caroline and said, "First, we should tell you that we are not having dinner here tonight. I made reservations for all of us at Stonewood, at the Country Club. I reserved a private dining room. There will be eleven of us, and we won't meet them until eight o'clock."

"What about Siggy? Is she all right?" asked Caroline.

"She is fine, a knot on her head maybe, but she's fine," responded Carmen.

"Who else is coming?"

"Jackson Greene, JB Robles, and Robbie Collicci," said Carmen, smiling at her husband. "It will be a good distraction to have these handsome men at the table tonight. Robbie said he would drive the guest van, so that will take care of the others. The three of us can drive together."

"Good, then we have time to talk," said Caroline. She also thought that with added guests, the dinner conversation might go in a more comfortable direction. There would be no discussion of the previous night.

"First, what happened at the school?" she asked.

"There was another fire, but it wasn't arson this time. It looks like lightning struck nearby. There was a power surge, and something electrical blew up and started a fire inside the school. Probably someone left a computer on and it exploded," explained JB.

"What are they going to do?" asked Caroline.

"We'll be having a full council meeting on Sunday night to figure that out. We've invited the parents, too," answered Carmen. "By then, most of our company of women friends should be on their way back home."

"I hope your meeting goes well and you can move forward quickly," said Caroline. "I want you to know that I met with Robbie Collicci this morning, while you were gone. He revealed many things about Frank that I had not known before. I'm not ready to talk about all of them, but one thing I *will* tell you...was that Frank was planning to give you the AngelFire Inn when we retired."

JB and Carmen Robles jaws dropped and they did not even try to respond.

"You are both on notice that I am planning to honor Frank's wishes and do the same," added Caroline.

In addition to their dropped jaws, a tear began to roll down each of their faces. Again, they did not even try to respond. Each sat in suspended animation.

Caroline continued unabated, "Also, I've prepared these checks for you, as bonuses. It would have been impossible for me to have run the Inn without the two of you this past year." She handed them separate envelopes, with checks inside, each made out for twenty-five thousand dollars.

Upon opening the envelope, Carmen turned and grabbed her husband's arm, to steady herself. Their eyes met and they were finally able to speak. Mr. and Mrs. Robles still in amazement, eyes brimming with tears, spoke in unison, "Now we can help with the new school."

"I would also like to help with the new school," Caroline said, without skipping a beat, and with full confidence, "Who knows, perhaps Nicole and Paula may possibly teach there and be a valued part of the faculty. If not, we'll help them some other way. I will make sure that you will have a state of the art school for the reservation."

Carmen at last, centered herself and turned to Caroline. "Wait a minute, Caroline this could cost a great deal of money, even *millions*. I don't understand. Do you know what you are saying?" asked Carmen.

"Carmen, it seems that I now *have* millions, tens and tens of millions. Apparently my husband had another lucrative business that generated this money over the past twenty years. For some reason, I have yet to understand, he did not want to reveal this fortune to me. So for the past twenty years, he has only invested and reinvested it.

I will tell you that apparently, the Amoroso family and the Collicci family are in the business of manufacturing slot machines and various other gaming equipment. Frank arranged meetings with the New Mexico and Arizona tribes, who were exploring the possibilities of building casinos, and his "family tribe", furnished the equipment. Frank made obscene commissions on these dealings. The rest I'll share with you after our guests leave.

In the meantime, I'll help fund the school, and we'll also discuss the future of the AngelFire Inn, next week. Please let's keep this between us. I'm not sure I want this to go public yet, or maybe, ever. So nothing tonight, and on Sunday, at your meeting, please say you have an anonymous benefactor."

As hard as they tried...words to describe their gratitude were most difficult to find.

Dinner at Eight for Eleven

"I'd like to be the sort of friend that you have been to me
I'd like to be the help that you've been always glad to be;
I'd like to mean as much to you each minute of the day
As you have meant, old friends of mine, to me along the way"

Edgar A. Guest

J B, unconscious of his perpetual smile, drove Caroline's
Volvo over to the Country Club. Carmen was beaming, but
Caroline was distracted and still a bit dazed. The puzzle
of Frank's return had just begun to be solved yet it still left questions no one would be able to answer. Perhaps, not even Frank
himself. She had lost him twice, and her gut was aching. Tonight
would be a good diversion, and she was determined to muster up
heartfelt smiles for the friends she loved so dearly. She needed
this evening to be a success. For them, for herself.

When they arrived, the maître d' escorted them to the dining room where the evening began with a long process of sincere
embraces and well wishes. Each guest stood on the precipice of

change; all of them with hope. Caroline's friends were pleased to see her gracious smile, and were sensitive to the courage it took for her to finish the week with them.

"Well Jackson Greene," greeted Caroline. "Aren't you a beautiful sight?"

"Hello, Caroline," replied Jackson. Holding both of her hands in his, he said, "I'm so glad to be here. It's wonderful to be back at AngelFire. Diana told me how supportive you have been this week. Thank you, I appreciate all that you have done for her, and for us."

"Did Diana take you to that gorgeous mountain today? It's a sacred place, Jackson," said Caroline.

"She did, and we hadn't been up there together in a long time. It was truly a beautiful experience for both of us," replied Jackson.

Caroline gave Diana's hand a squeeze, and they exchanged glances that assured Caroline that things were going well.

Caroline turned and saw Siggy. She held her for a silent moment and said, "Please tell me you're okay."

"Oh, of course I am...Katie was right. There was nothing seriously wrong with me at all," she answered. "The worst thing is, I will have to limit my trips to high altitudes."

"Dr. Katie," Caroline began. "I am so grateful to you for all you did for Siggy." As she placed her arm around Kate's shoulders, she whispered, "And for me and Frank." Fighting back tears, they quickly turned away from each other.

Then Caroline noticed Robbie. "Mr. Collicci," she started, then turned to the others, and said, "Everyone please....meet my new best friend Robbie, as it seems." She leaned over and whispered to him, "And brother-in-law...thank you ... I'm glad you're here." Robbie looked as if he was unsure of what to expect from Caroline, and was pleased with her graciousness.

Marti gave a quizzical glance toward Diana, and shrugged her shoulders. Both women appeared equally curious as to this "new best friend" relationship. Siggy missed the comment all together, but Paula and Nicole looked at each other, a little puzzled. No one asked for an explanation. There would be no serious discussions this evening.

Caroline still had many questions. Frank clearly had trusted Robbie, and she decided she would trust him too. *God, I wish Frank were here tonight*, she thought. *He would have been such a great host...well, never mind.* She took a deep breath and moved on.

When she approached Marti, she leaned over and said, "I'll need your help tomorrow morning."

"Done," replied Marti. There was nothing one would not do for the other.

Hors d'oeuvres had already been placed on the table. Both red and white New Mexico wines were delivered. Savory soups were followed by lobster salads. Entrees of regional favorites were served with corn cakes and sopapillas.

The conversations were kept to agreeable subjects and light-hearted teasing. Nicole and Paula were having a wonderful time and both were completely at ease. All diners took pleasure in the food, the ambiance, and the good company.

"There surely is a difference in the conversation when men are at the table," Carmen whispered to Caroline, who laughed at her observation.

"You're right; until tonight, we haven't spoken of sports, politics or the stock market all week!"

With a sigh of contentment, from the pleasure of a good meal, Paula said, "I have never eaten New Mexican food before. I don't understand why it is kept like some kind of a national secret. The whole country knows Maine lobster, Boston clam chowder, Iowa corn and Idaho potatoes..."

Siggy added, "Or New York cheesecake, Chicago pizza..."

Nicole added, "Seattle coffees...Wisconsin cheese."

"Don't forget the California wine country, where I live," added Kate.

When the dessert menus were provided, Caroline addressed the waiter, "Sir, please tell me, do you have those wonderful little Symphony Sweets? You know those little two-bite pies?"

"Why, no Ma'am. I'm not sure I am aware of them. Please tell me more?" he asked.

"A company called Symphony Sweets, or something like that, makes them. They really are a delicious and visually dazzling dessert," declared Caroline.

And with that announcement the crowd burst into praise and applause for Siggy. She smiled the biggest smile her face would give, and her eyes welled up with tears. "You liked them? You really liked them?" It was all she could say for the moment.

"Yes, *Sally*, we really liked them," said Marti as she stood and held up her glass to lead the others in a toast, "To my dear friend Siggy...we have been your taste testers and guinea pigs, for years and years, and um...years! Tonight, we forgive you for all the curious creations which came before last night. When Carmen uncovered that beautiful tray, we all knew this was IT! This was what you have been waiting for. Your creativity has taken you to a new level, even if it is your grandma's pies, we will all think of it as Siggy's Symphony Sweets. Sometimes you don't have to create something unheard of, or untested, but to simply make a great improvement on something that is already good. Surely Siggy, this is just the beginning! Congratulations!"

Siggy tried to speak in response, but when she opened her mouth, the words would not come. The vivacious, gregarious Siggy, cleared her throat, her voice cracked, and she said, "Thank you, all of you. I know that it may have seemed like an endurance trial, but I am thrilled to have your unanimous approval *on something!* "

A variety of Stonewood's delectable desserts were placed around the table along with coffees, teas and aperitifs. As the diners shared and sampled the desserts, Caroline looked around the table and took in a moment of contentment. The events of the previous night were set aside, just as she had hoped. She took pleasure in watching her friends finding joy in just being together. Their annual retreat was nearly over, and with the exception of Carmen; each of her friends had stood at a crossroads and had made a commitment to a new direction for her life. The last year had been a painful one for Caroline. What would this next year bring for her, especially now?

JB signed for the bill, which was charged to the AngelFire Inn, and Caroline noticed for the first time, how in yet another way, JB had been filling Frank's shoes over the past year.

As for JB, all he wanted was to be alone with Carmen and he was ready to go home. His mind was still swirling with Caroline's news. His amorous glances toward Carmen throughout the dinner were mirrored in her responsive eyes.

Amid warm hearts and laughter, Robbie Collicci gathered his flock and shepherded them back to the AngelFire Inn. Mr. and Mrs. Robles, along with their newly declared benefactor, returned to their AngelFire home in a more pensive state. Their minds were spinning with past, present and future – thoughts, dreams, regrets and mysteries. Not to mention, Frank or last night.

Once at the Inn, the three of them agreed to meet again in the morning before breakfast. Caroline took the long climb up the staircase to her apartment. She turned on the hot water and prepared for a long soak in her steeping tub. There would be no music tonight. No calling out to her metaphysical lover. Instead, there would be plans and decisions to be made.

The Determined Launch

"Only a life lived for others is worth living."

~ Albert Einstein

*C*aroline began her day at six o'clock in the morning with a brisk walk to the lake. On her return trip, she found Nicole and Paula on the trail in a vigorous ascent, panting breathlessly.

"Good morning!" said Caroline. Although merely hanging by the threads of her emotions, she was steadfast in her intent to remain in good spirits. She carried on, "Enjoy your walk, and I'll see you at breakfast." They nodded, and she kept her pace and they kept theirs. When she arrived at the Inn, JB and Carmen were waiting for her in the kitchen.

Carmen handed her a cup of coffee and invited her to sit with them in the breakfast nook. Caroline braced herself for whatever was coming next.

JB spoke first. "Caroline, we want to talk to you about the money, about the Inn, and about Frank. We know you must have been in shock yesterday when you learned of Frank's business dealings and the fortunes he kept from you. We don't know why he did this, but we do know how he loved you and AngelFire. We both know this is true. We think there is a possibility that you wrote those two checks yesterday while still in shock, and we brought them with us this morning to give them back to you."

"We love this place, but we love *you* more. There is no need for you to ever turn it over to us. We wouldn't want to run it without you," explained Carmen. She continued, conveying her sentiments, which were matched by her husband's.

"Now, I want to talk to you about the school..." said JB. He took a deep breath, but before he could say a word, Caroline interrupted, "Stop. Please just stop. You are the only two people I know who would stand by me day after day during this miserable year and try to create some kind of 'new normal' for me as I *walked into walls* around here. In this past year, my family and my friends all had good ideas and advice about what I should do – next or never. No one, not even Julia this time, stood by me as did the two of you. You quietly helped me through my grief with patience, understanding and support; all the while going through your own grief. And, on top of it all, kept the Inn running, as if nothing happened. For some inexplicable reason, that was a feat I had not fully grasped until this week.

This money is giving me an opportunity to give back to you. As for the school, it is a good investment in the community. All we ever really have in life is each other, and it is my intention to share with you what is now, my good fortune. Robbie is fully aware of the commitments I made yesterday, and he will support these decisions. He made no objections to my plans and I trust his judgment. I will not make any financial decisions without him. So both of you – just take those checks and go to the bank! Call Robbie if you need some advice. I will, however, need you back here this afternoon to meet with Nicole and Paula. You will need to prepare them for tomorrow's meeting with your board and the parents of the students. And please remember, I am just an anonymous benefactor.

I will talk to Nicole and Paula after breakfast. I'm sure that they can be helpful advisors.

In the meantime, I need to shower and change for breakfast. I'll cook this morning."

"Uh...I already made breakfast for everyone. You just need to heat up part of it," said Carmen.

"Still don't trust me in the kitchen, do you?" asked Caroline.

"Nope," Carmen answered smiling. After reiterated expressions of gratitude, Carmen and JB left for their bank in Taos.

When fully prepared for the day, Caroline was resolute to generate some amazing opportunities, so she went to the Internet and started with making travel arrangements.

At eight-thirty, she heard Marti call out to her from the kitchen, at the bottom of the stairs. "Come on up, I'm in my office," invited Caroline. Marti came in with two cups of coffee. "Don't you look professional this morning? How long have you been up?"

"A few hours, and I still have several calls to make. I've been on the Internet for the last hour, at least. I have a project for you, and it needs to be kept confidential. I've made a list of people I'd like you to call this morning from your bungalow." She handed Marti the lists. "Page two defines your objective. We'll make an offer today. Call me if you have any questions or get any answers. I don't want her to know about this just in case it doesn't work out. Then, we can create a *Plan 'B'*."

Marti perused the list on page one and quickly skipped to page two. She radiated with joy. "I don't know if we can pull this off, but it's a great idea. I'll get right on it. By the way, it's possible that Diana and Jackson may be leaving today. It's something about a scheduled event." Marti was excited about her task at hand and promptly returned to her bungalow.

Caroline's next call was to Robbie Collicci. She told him of her intentions, and he told her of his. She gave him his assignments, and after a brief discussion, they were in agreement. She closed the door to make another call, this one...to a man she hadn't spoken to in over thirty years.

While at Stonewood, all guests had agreed that a late breakfast was in order for Saturday morning. The two servers, scheduled by JB, arrived at nine o'clock to assist Caroline. They arranged bowls of fresh fruits, heated the quiches that Carmen had prepared, and presented individual servings of homemade yoghurt. Carmen had even bought blueberry muffins from the local bakery, which were certain to be a crowd pleaser.

All guests with the exception of Marti and Jackson arrived for breakfast by ten o'clock. Seven envelopes were placed at the seven place settings. Each was scripted with a name and marked *"Please Do Not Open Until Noon."*

Caroline took on her *gracious host demeanor*, a well-honed skill from her past, which she had learned during her marriage to Ric Roberts, the politico. *I could have been a great actress*, she used to tell him. No matter what was going on in her personal life, she had to be gracious at political events, for her husband's sake. This was different. She loved these guests, and the deal-making about to happen here was not for votes, not for political power. The act was not just merely to conceal her pain but to begin to transform it through the role of benefactor. *How long could one feel sorrow in that role?* She would sponsor someone else's dreams, for she had none left of her own...for now.

Diana sat next to Caroline and made it known that things were going well between her and Jackson. "Progress, we're making progress," she sighed softly. "He's in the bungalow making calls, trying to arrange for an earlier return flight. He is taping a show tomorrow morning."

"Well, are *you* ready to leave, Diana? You know that you may stay as long as you like," said Caroline.

"Have you decided whether this issue was a moment or a behavior?" asked Kate softly, as she sat down next to Diana.

"I want to believe it was a moment of madness," she answered. "Time will answer this question. Not since the birth of our first baby girl, have I seen him this humble."

"Will you be able to get away together?" asked Nicole. "It may help. It surely made a difference this week for us!" Nicole placed her hand over Paula's, and they exchanged tender glances. It was obvious that they were in agreement of their plans to stay in New Mexico.

"I'm not sure we can go anywhere right now. We just bought and furnished our new home. It may not be practical." Diana lamented, "The truth is...I haven't brought it up."

Caroline saw the discomfort in Diana's eyes and changed the subject. "Nicole and Paula, will you be free to meet with Carmen and JB later this afternoon? They are going to a council meeting tomorrow about the high school. It would be a good time for you to meet some of the school board members."

"Of course!" said the doppelgangers. "We'd love to!"

Halfway through the breakfast, Marti walked in and joined her friends. She slipped a note to Caroline, which read, *"We need to talk a.s.a.p."* She filled her plate from the buffet, saw the envelope with her name on it, and looked quizzically at Caroline. She looked around the table and noticed that everyone else had an envelope, and assumed it was one of Caroline's fancy invitations to this year's farewell dinner.

"These muffins are wonderful," said Siggy. "I could have made some muffins for this breakfast. I have loads of good recipes."

"Indeed you do, and we have already eaten each and every one of them," taunted Marti. "I think my favorites were the muffins with the frozen peas and corn in them. *Those* were healthy."

"How about if you just stick to those wonderful little pies," said Kate. "We all loved them. It was like a holiday preview, and I don't think we even saved one for you!"

"Thank you Katie. You've been a real angel for me on this trip. I am feeling so much better. I was absolutely terrified in that helicopter! I was sure one of us was going to fall out of that thing. And you were right – Altitude Sickness! Who would have thought, after all these years of coming up to these mountains?"

"Siggy, none of us are getting any younger, and our body chemistry keeps changing. Fun, isn't it?" said Kate. "I would like to take a look at your stitches after breakfast, if you don't mind."

Siggy silently nodded in agreement, slightly embarrassed by the bandage on her forehead.

"We're just glad everything turned out so well," added Caroline. "Katie, what's your plan for today?"

"Well, since I'm leaving tomorrow morning, I would like to see Robbie tonight, unless you have something planned. I guess I'll pack this afternoon," replied Kate.

"Carmen and JB will return this afternoon, and we are preparing for a wonderful evening with entertainment and no doubt another delectable dinner. Please invite Robbie to join us. We'll check in with each other for how many will be having lunch at the lake today, as some of the staff are here and will prepare box lunches."

And then Caroline addressed the entire group...

"In the meantime, your mission is to read the instructions inside your envelopes, at noon."

Notes to My Friends

"A friend may well be reckoned the masterpiece of nature."

- Ralph Waldo Emerson

*P*aula and Nicole returned to their bungalow to continue their research for teaching jobs in New Mexico. Nicole seized the laptop computer and began to revise her resume. At the stroke of 12:00 noon, Paula opened her note.

Dear Paula,

First, I wish to echo the sentiments given by Carmen at dinner on Thursday evening as you join our company of friends. I hope that since you've expressed your desire to stay in New Mexico, we will have the opportunity to enjoy a lovely friendship. Life has been beautiful for me in AngelFire, and although the winters are cold and the snow is deep, I expect its beauty may surpass winters in Chicago.

By now, you know that AngelFire has no schools of its own and the closest are in Red River. As a resort town, we have a very small year round population. From what I've heard from Nicole, you are a brilliant musician and, most recently, created an award winning music program. Your students in Chicago will no doubt miss you.

Your task today is to write down your ideal situation. What do you dream of? I ask you to do this and hope that you will be willing to share this with me at 1:30 pm in my office.

Your next step, should you decide to proceed, will be revealed to you then.

Caroline

Diana brought a breakfast tray back to her bungalow for Jackson. As she walked in, he was just finishing a phone call. "Well it looks like I can get a ticket on your flight tomorrow, but there is nothing available for today. I called Reverend Thomas, who will speak for me tomorrow −which should be interesting," said Jackson. He walked over to Diana and embraced her. Reluctantly, she responded. Her heart still ached and her mind was still racing. If everything Jackson had told her was true, they were about to embark upon a whole new chapter in their marriage. *How long would it take for me to really trust him*, she wondered. In an instant, she had lost faith in him and questioned the strength of their marriage. Yet, reversal of her heartache could not happen in an instant. For Diana, the immediate answer was prayer.

She handed Jackson the envelope from Caroline, as she opened hers at 12:05 pm.

"What's this?" he queried.

"I don't know. We all had one on our plates at breakfast, and we were asked not to open them until noon," she answered, and walked into the bedroom to read hers in private.

Dear Diana,

To no one's surprise, but everyone's continued admiration, you have handled your crisis this week with dignity and grace. Whatever happens with you and Jackson, the ministry, or your ministry, please know that I will support you in any way I possibly can.

I've experienced a new level of my own pain this week, and only hope I can mirror your character. I have received news this week, which I have not yet spoken of at our gatherings. I wish to speak with you at 12:30 pm, if possible. I will explain, then.
Caroline

"What is it?" Jackson asked Diana when she came back into the room.

"I have to go see Caroline in a few minutes. I hope she is all right. She's been quiet and a little distant since Thursday night. She says she has something important to tell me. Did you open yours, yet?"

"I'll do it right now." He looked at his watch like a man who lives by it. His cell phone rang again, for the fifth time that morning. He took the call and left the envelope lying on the table next to him. Diana went to freshen up, looked into the mirror, and noticed the frown on her face. *We have created a very complicated existence,* she thought, and wondered, *is this really fixable?*

At 12:25 pm, Diana walked out of the bungalow. Jackson Greene was conducting business as usual. So many details to running this organization, yet it was good work that helped a great many people. The envelope was still on the table, unopened.

Inside it said....

Dear Jackson,
I cannot tell you how pleased I am at your return to Angel-Fire. It was wonderful to be able to laugh together again last night at Stonewood. I hope you will relax and enjoy what little time you have to spend here at Mother Nature's summer retreat. Whatever happens next for you, know that you are always held in my highest regard.

I wish to share something important with you and ask that you come to my office at 12:45pm.
Caroline

Marti had been on the telephone in her bungalow, following through with Caroline's requests. Not only was she making calls on Siggy's behalf for business, but also for her family. She called Siggy's daughter, Sherry, for the third time as well.

Marti was a wizard with details and had gathered an extraordinary amount of information in a very short time. Her son Erik also made a few additional calls to his contacts in Los Angeles. They were a good team – always had been. As a single mom, Marti often masked her loneliness through her devotion to her son. As he became his own man, she expressed most of it through her music. Now, in her silence, she faced a turning point, one she had only dreamed of. Standing at these crossroads, she was as frightened as she had ever been.

Marti detected a note of mystery when she found one of Caroline's notes had also been at her place setting. She opened her note at 12:15 pm.

Dear Marti,

What a week this has been! As always you are there by my side when I need you the most. Through the storms of my life, your support has ferried me to the shores of safety and sanity.

I wish to thank you for your willingness to gather important information for me today. If there is anyone who can pull this together, it is you.

I also want to acknowledge how hard it was for you to reveal the truth about Erik this week, after all these years. You know that Kate, Julia and I would have taken your secret to the grave. Please accept my continued support in taking this to the next step.

I would like to have you here with me in the office, when we do the "big reveal." You are the right person to give the news. So please come to my office at 2:00 pm and we'll take the next step.
    Caroline

Kate was on the telephone too, but it was a game of tag with Robbie. His last message said he was working with clients and would likely be with them most of the morning. She was last to leave the "*You're it*" message. She decided to take a long, hot soak in the tub and think. What a great week this had been. Kate had come to AngelFire to rest and re-establish communications with women friends she cared about deeply. Her clinic had become so incredibly demanding that she barely kept in contact beyond the usual birthday/Christmas cards and gifts. She regretted that her phone calls to Caroline this year were too infrequent. She knew better.

Then there was Robbie Collicci; this man she had just met, who felt so familiar, so comfortable. After such a beautiful experience with him, could she just get on a plane tomorrow and say "*Bye, See Ya!*" *Is it true you can fall in love in a week?* How does one carry on a relationship with a man who lives thirteen hundred miles away?

She opened her envelope at 12:20 pm.

Dear Katie,

Who would have thought our retreat would have turned into such an extraordinary week!

You probably thought you were coming here to relax! I cannot find the words to convey my gratitude for your support in my final experience with Frank. The last goodbye was the hardest.

I know you are struggling to define your relationship with Robbie Collicci. He is a good friend, who I believe to be a good man. He has shared with me his feelings for you, and I believe this relationship is worth pursuing. What does your heart tell you? Your wisdom has helped all of us and now it's my turn to help you.

Let us discuss this, in my office at 3:00 pm. I think I know how...
Caroline

Nicole finished the update of her resume and continued on to the Internet job search. Most of the opportunities were in rural districts, with the exception of a position as a secondary math teacher at the Academy for Technology & the Classics, a charter school in Santa Fe. The position intrigued her. One problem appeared to be the logistical demand of both math and music positions in the same city. Whether or not she and Paula were at the same school was no longer relevant. This situation deemed further discussions regarding their future.

She presumed Caroline's notes were well wishes for a future in New Mexico.

At 12:30, she opened it and read....

Dear Niki,

Well, here we are at another pivot in the dance of life. We're both performing our turns and are twirling to the best of our ability. But where exactly are we going? Do we ever really know the answer to that question? I'm dizzy just thinking about it!

I would very much like to speak with you about opportunities here in New Mexico. Please chasse over to my office at 1:00 pm and bring your ideas, your concerns, and your dreams. Let's see what we can work out together.

Caroline

Siggy was beginning to pack boxes of pots, baking supplies and pans, when she decided to drop everything and call her daughter, Sherry. After the fourth ring, she blurted, "Sherry, it's mom. I want to apologize again for the accident in your kitchen. I hope someday you will forgive me. I had another fainting spell here in AngelFire, while hiking on the mountain with my friends. Your Aunt Katie and I were airlifted by helicopter to a hospital in Taos. It was quite a trip! After a number of tests, they concluded that I was suffering from altitude sickness. I now know I don't do well at high altitudes, which I guess you may already know. Anyway, please don't be mad at me too long this time. I miss my granddaughters." She was talking to Sherry's voicemail.

Siggy finished packing another box, wiped her eyes, blew her nose, and opened Caroline's note.

Dear Siggy,

What a dramatic week! Your fiery entrance with Sherry, the helicopter ride to a Taos hospital, and for the grand finale, Symphony Sweets! Congratulations! We are all holding good thoughts for your future.

I know there is much for you to think about. If you really do indeed want your 'Sweets' career, what's next? Perhaps I can help you make some decisions. Please come to my office at 2:00 pm, so we can discuss your ideas and dreams.

Caroline

Time

"What do we live for, if it is not to make life less difficult for each other?"

- George Eliot

aroline was fully prepared. Six files were placed on her desk, labeled with six names of her treasured friends. At the knock on the door, she took a deep breath and opened it, and then closed it behind her first guest.

Diana arrived precisely on time at twelve-thirty. She was, as usual, beautifully dressed, coifed and manicured, but looked tired and drawn. She sat down and leaned forward toward Caroline's desk. "How are you feeling, Caroline? I know you've been through a lot this week, probably more than you ever dreamed of, so please tell me, are you feeling all right about what's happened? I mean... is there anything I can do for you?"

"Well, this is not how I thought this meeting would start," replied Caroline. "I'm doing my best. I'm trying to stay present and do what's in front of me. I would rather focus on how things are going with you and Jackson."

"Well, like I said this morning, we are making progress. The trip up to the mountain was inspiring for both of us. I poured out my feelings and I felt that he heard me. He begged me to trust his word. It was the deepest conversation we've had about our marriage in years. We both have taken a lot for granted. No one really knows or understands how hard we work.

He spoke of his love for me as sincerely as ever. Yet, I am still unsure of myself. I want to believe him, and well...I guess this will take some time," said Diana.

"What was his version of what happened?" asked Caroline.

"He told me that on that day, he had received a couple of messages from Miss Elaina, that new organist. He had not returned her calls because there is a protocol for these things. Questions are left with his administrator Georgia, who will then get answers, and return most of the calls for him. He said that Georgia handed him her messages and said *'watch out for that one'*. Normally, he trusts Georgia's intuition.

The story goes, that he went to look for Miss Elaina to reaffirm this policy, but could not find her in the choir rehearsal room. He heard noises coming from the choir's wardrobe room and went in to investigate. When Miss Elaina saw him, she burst into tears professing some personal family drama. Jackson said he *'touched her arm'* to console her, and the next thing he knew she had thrown her full body at him, which is just when I walked into the room. He said that he pushed her away – which must have happened when I turned and ran. He said that he fired her, right on the spot. She packed up her things and left within the hour. Georgia escorted Miss Elaina to her car," reported Diana. "Jackson said that when he found the financial papers on the floor, he knew I had been in the room and he started calling me immediately."

"Do you believe him?" asked Caroline. "You left out the kiss, Diana."

"Well, I called Georgia, and she backed him up one hundred percent. She said he even asked her to be part of the hiring process from now on," added Diana. "I think it was a "moment" as we spoke of on Monday, nonetheless, perhaps a defining moment.

It has made me take a look at everything we have created, how complicated it has become, and how it has changed us. It takes up all our time and energy. There's not been much time left just for the two of us. The good thing is that we both still love what we do – and each other."

"So, what's next?" Caroline inquired. *She still left out the kiss*, she thought.

"Well first, I haven't told him that I want to be a visible part of the TV Ministry. I think I have something to offer, and I also think that people would like to see a dedicated couple that works as a team. I know it seems ironic that I say this in the middle of a marriage crisis."

"Seems?" stated Caroline. "Perhaps the marriage needs to be repaired or restored, first. Then you can present what really is – the truth. As long as *you think* you are *'in the middle of a marriage crisis'* you can't possibly be authentic. Don't underestimate the perceptions of your audience. What if you come out on the other side of this crisis? Would you want a ministry of your own?"

"I can't even think about that as a possibility," answered Diana.

"What are your options, Diana? Would you go back to North Carolina and pretend that everything is okay? Just practice damage control and hope that this all gets smoothed over?" Caroline looked at the clock, which read 12:45 pm. "Did you give Jackson his note?"

"Why yes, I did...Why?" asked Diana.

"He is supposed to be joining us right now. I have something to say to him, to both of you actually. Where do you think he is?" Caroline asked.

"Most likely, he's on his cell phone. It is his constant companion. Jackson has become a *techie* and always has to have the latest communication technology. I think it's harmless, and frankly, I'm grateful he doesn't want a motorcycle or a convertible sports car," said Diana, somewhat defensively.

"Maybe we should try calling him. I have a schedule to keep today," Caroline said.

She turned to get her telephone, but there was a knock at the door. Jackson came in the door at 12:49 pm.

"Sorry ladies, I was talking to Reverend Thomas about his presentation for tomorrow," he said as he leaned over to kiss Diana. "So what can I do for the two of you?"

Caroline spoke first, "For the first time, Jackson, I am here to do something for you. You stood by me when I had marital problems with Ric, and last year you greatly assisted me with the memorial service for Frank. I know that you've remained good friends with Ric and on occasion have counseled my sons. We're like family Jackson, and we've gone through several chapters in our lives that will not be forgotten. What happened to Ric and me is not all that unlike what you and Diana are facing today."

Jackson leaned forward and interrupted Caroline, "Just a minute Caroline, what has happened here was a misunderstanding, and the timing was such that Diana missed the truth."

"Really Jackson? I think you are missing out on the facts *and* the truth," asserted Caroline. "Don't you remember what the problems were with Ric and me? He was so focused on his political campaigns that there was no room for *us*. He was either in a meeting or on the telephone, or the computer, or dealing with any number of distractions. I didn't know how to get past my resentments about it, and I wasn't very gracious about it either. The point I really want to get to Jackson – is about TIME. During those last few years, Ric and I had so little of it together; that I think the lack of it – is what destroyed us. And, we didn't know how to fix it.

TIME is what I had with Frank. We had AngelFire to work on together, just as you and Diana have your ministry to work on together. We loved what we did here and the people we served, just as you love your ministry and the people you serve. We spent most of our time aware of *how* we loved each other. We had twelve of the happiest, most romantic years of my adult life. I want all my friends to experience the depth of love and the degree of happiness that we shared.

So Jackson, you must understand why I am so sensitive to TIME; because, within minutes *Frank's TIME* was over...finished forever. I urge you to take TIME seriously.

From what I have observed, you are not that much different from Ric, who is still a hard-working man with a cause, just like you. He *and* you have allowed yourselves to get swallowed up by the undercurrent of your work. Without you even noticing, it has eroded the quality of the life you and Diana have together.

Without a doubt, this can be a pivotal time for both of you. You can move forward together or you can go back to Raleigh and stay swimming upstream – until you drown in your cause.

Jackson, I am proposing that you consider calling your board of directors and telling them you need some time off and want them to play *re-runs* on your TV show. I'm also suggesting that your associate ministers handle the day-to-day duties of your ministry, with your administrator Georgia, who is probably capable of running the whole place anyway. And, I'm asking you to do this for a full month. You need a vacation, both of you. You need TIME.

TIME to heal; TIME for love; TIME to remember; TIME to look to the future; and to make a new plan. TIME to remember the Diana and Jackson, I met so many years ago."

Jackson and Diana simultaneously responded, "A month? We appreciate your concern Caroline. That really sounds wonderful but we can't possibly...."

Caroline raised her right hand to halt their reply and said, "I am handing you TIME." She removed a large manila envelope from a file and handed it over to them. They opened it together. The contents of the envelope revealed computer generated airline tickets for two and reservations for a month at the Renaissance Hotel in the British Virgin Islands. Faxed receipts were marked PAID IN FULL. In addition, there were vouchers and American Express gift checks. "It won't cost you a thing but your TIME. It's an offer...think about it. You can let me know later. Seriously, think about this and consider it a gift from someone who loves you both, very much."

Diana and Jackson sat agape and wordless. They looked at each other, then back to Caroline. "Where...How... What...?" started Diana, shaking her head.

Caroline began, "Apparently, the Frank Amoroso I *didn't* have the TIME to get to know, has left me a not-so-small fortune, which has allowed me to do some very lovely things for my friends. Believe me, what I have just given you, is a just a nominal part of it.

Now, you two have some calls to make, and I have another appointment. Go —I love you both."

Choices

"Get not your friends by bare compliments, but by giving them sensible tokens of your love."

- Socrates

*T*he door was half way open when Nicole walked in. Caroline was wiping her eyes, trying to maintain her composure. She put away a file and centered the second one on her desk.

"Hey, Caroline...is there something I can do? Are you all right?" Nicole asked.

"I'm fine. Actually, those were some happy tears for a change," Caroline said. "So Niki, how do you feel about living here in New Mexico?"

"I think it is beautiful here, just as Paula does. We may do very well here, as long as we can get some good medical care for her. I know that all of New Mexico doesn't look like AngelFire, and over the next two weeks, we'll need to traverse the state and decide where we'd like to settle."

"That's right, from desert to mountain tops – it's all here. Have you updated your resume or started a job search?" asked Caroline.

"I did, and actually found an opening in a Santa Fe charter school that looks interesting. It's a good fit for me, but they have no position open for Paula. It appears we won't be teaching at the same school anymore," said Nicole.

"Tell me Niki, what would be your most ideal situation," asked Caroline. "If you could do anything at all, what would it be?"

"What would really interest me is creating and producing a multi-media program that would inspire children to explore the mathematical landscapes of the universe, and to unlock the codes of nature. To understand that we live in an era based on technology and that the options can be limitless, but that they must have good math skills to compete. It is the only way we can be successful in a global world economy. Kids today have amazing computer skills, but need the science and math behind them to create their own futures," said Nicole. She took the next twelve minutes to communicate her ideas about the program in technological terms of which Caroline had absolutely no understanding.

Just when her eyes were about to glaze over, Caroline said, "Well, Professor Roberts, it sounds like you've put a great deal of thought into this. Have you ever proposed this to a school board?"

"With school budget cuts nationwide, it's unlikely there will be money for anything like this for at least, the next decade. I've also found that there are too few good teaching jobs available here in New Mexico, and I hear the drop-out rate is distressing," said Nicole.

"What if I were able to find you some private money for this math program of yours?" proposed Caroline. "How long would it take you to put this together?"

Nicole sat up straight and looked quizzically at Caroline. "Not having any media resources established yet, I would say at least a year," said Nicole, wondering where this conversation was going.

"I have another question. I have arranged for you and Paula to meet with Carmen and JB at 2:00 pm. I don't know if you have heard about it yet, but the school on the reservation in Taos was destroyed by fire on Thursday night, and they are working with their Council to try to build a new one before winter. They may want to talk to you about teaching, or about becoming an advisor to lead this school into the twenty-first century. Would you be interested in that project?" Caroline offered.

"Sounds fascinating! I would love to be a part of building a new school."

"What about Paula? Do you think she would be interested?"

"The new rule is that I try not to speak for Paula; however, I think enthusiastic nodding may be permitted," joked Nicole. "Has she been invited to that meeting?"

"Yes, and any moment now, she should be here, and I want you to stay in the room. I have some options I'd like you both to consider, together," said Caroline.

"Caroline, I am so grateful...," started Nicole.

"That's what sisters do, Niki," said Caroline. "Isn't that what you used to say to me, all those times when you picked up the boys for some Roberts family event, when their father wasn't available? It's my turn, that's all...it's just my turn."

A rhythmic tap on the door indicated that indeed Paula had arrived. She wore the same jeans as Nicole, same tank top – in a different color. Caroline wondered how much aware they were of their "sameness". For some odd reason, it seemed unspoken. She welcomed Paula and informed her of her intent to keep Nicole in this meeting. "Before we begin – Since neither of you are working right now, where do you stand on health insurance?"

As usual, Nicole spoke first, "We're covered for the next thirty days, and then we either get coverage through other jobs or arrange for coverage through a Cobra plan. The question is, should we need it, will our health insurance be accepted here in New Mexico?"

"Let's make this easy. On Monday morning, I will add the both of you to our employee health plan, here at AngelFire," said Caroline. "We'll work out all the details next week. I can keep you both working here until you find teaching jobs...if of course, that's okay with you."

"Now, Paula, what would be your ideal work situation?"

Paula smiled and said, "Ideally? I would love to stay right here, but since there are no schools in AngelFire, that's not an option.

You asked for my dreams Caroline, so here it is...In a perfect world every school district would have youth orchestras that are so great they would perform internationally, inspiring other children to make music a part of their lives and exchanging styles and methods with other children in other countries.

Music programs are in crisis all over this country. I want to help kids who can't afford instruments or uniforms. I know many people who feel this way and would help, at least financially. Art and music department budgets have been slashed nationally, and I'd like to be part of the process that assures children a good education, which includes excellent musical training. And...that's it. I know I get pretty exuberant when I talk about it," she said apologetically.

Caroline picked up two of her files and placed them back down again. She squirmed a little in her chair, cleared her throat and then said, "Paula, I know you had much success with the youth orchestra at the school where you taught in Chicago. Forgive me, but I did a little research on you and your school competitions. The reason I did this was that Frank and I had as a regular guest here at AngelFire, who was conductor for the Albuquerque Youth Symphony. I called him today and faxed over to him everything I had downloaded from the Internet. He called me back...and well, he wants to meet with you, if you are interested. They have an opening for a conductor of the Albuquerque Youth Orchestra, which may be a better fit for you. He also faxed a package of information for you to review. It includes an application, schedules, and other details."

"If I am interested? In making a dream come true? Caroline, this could be a wonderful opportunity. How can I thank you?" Paula marveled. "Nicole, did you know about this?"

Nicole sat wide-eyed and closed mouthed, shaking her head '*No*'. She started to say something, but decided not to and held herself back.

"Niki," said Caroline. "You have a few choices. You can apply for the math and sciences teaching position at the Academy in Santa Fe, and/or possibly be an advisor for the school to be built in Taos – or start right away on your program to promote math and science education. After you meet with JB and Carmen, you can decide. For right now, you both are on the payroll here. We'll work out the details on that later. Don't worry...as I said, I'll be putting you both to work.

By the way, I know I am jumping a little ahead of myself here, but you both should know. I am unhappy to report that for reasons I don't quite understand, New Mexico schools do not pay their teachers enough, and it makes it tough for teachers to get ahead here. So when you lock in your new jobs, I would like to help you with housing. Nicole, do you remember that little village I used to live in called Placitas? It is a quiet, private little community halfway between Albuquerque and Santa Fe. The homes have a character and beauty that are a wonderful reflection of this Land of Enchantment we live in. It will give you a reasonable commute in either direction," said Caroline.

"Caroline, STOP! My head is spinning!" Nicole stood up and said, "Where is this coming from? Have you robbed a bank or won a lottery?"

"Oh, I'm sorry..." Caroline apologized. "I guess I didn't mention my news. I'm not exactly clear on all of the details yet, as I just found out about it yesterday, but it appears that my husband Frank was a very, very, wealthy man. I'm just sharing a small part of it with people I love. I want you to feel you have choices, options, and no need to worry. Is that all right? Was I too pushy? Or too strong?"

The pair sat silently for about five seconds. They first looked at each other, shrugged their shoulders, then simultaneously opened their mouths and said, "*Ooookay!*"

"Now, you have to go. You have a meeting in the dining room with Carmen and JB. Hopefully, you can help them."

Both women rose from their chairs, thanked Caroline profusely, and walked out the door, murmuring....

Sweet Trio

"True friendship is seen through the heart, not through the eyes."

~ Author Unknown

Caroline put two more files away and pulled two more to the center of the desk.

Marti entered the room smiling, after passing Nicole and Paula on the staircase. She had a file folder with her that she placed on Caroline's desk as she sat down. She mentioned seeing Nicole and Paula. "Those two seem happy," she noted. "You know, they look like they met at the annual Chicago twins' convention. Don't you think it's kind of odd that no one has said anything about that?"

"Not yet, anyway," commented Caroline. "So what do you have for me?"

"Take a look...I think we've found more than enough information to take care of her. Erik has friends in high places! My son never stops surprising me," said Marti.

"I'll bet he says the same about you," responded Caroline, as she perused the file. "Has he heard your latest composition?"

"Not yet," answered Marti. "I just finished it in time to meet the entry deadline."

"I know you are going to win this time. It's your turn, Marti. You've waited long enough. It's all going to happen for you; I just know it."

"I'm happy with my life either way, Caroline. My son is a wonderful man, who has a family that adores him. I have my music and am able to make a living doing what I love. I live in a nice house in a great city and I'm content. What more can I ask for?" said Marti.

Caroline looked up from the file she had been reading and commented on how thorough and organized it was. She knew she could count on Marti's resourcefulness.

"Have you started your letter to Erik's dad?" Caroline asked pointedly.

"Yes, I have," she answered. "About twelve times, and soon I will need a recycling bin in my bungalow."

"I know this is hard for you. You must have a hundred questions running through your mind," said Caroline compassionately.

"Yes, I do, and the first one is…why did I blurt this out the other night?" Marti said. "To change the subject, before Siggy gets here, do you think she is actually prepared to run a business?"

"I don't know. She's got a great product. It is a lot of work to make those tiny little pies and hand decorate each one. Carmen and I were trying to figure out what kind of pans she used and how long it took her to embellish them. Anyway, this should be a great opportunity for her," replied Caroline

"Or drive our whacky friend right over the edge," said Marti. "I hope she can handle this."

"We'll do everything we can to see that she succeeds," said Caroline.

"Since she and I still live fairly close to each other, I promise to keep an eye on her," said Marti.

"Eye on who?" asked Siggy as she entered the office wearing a bright red Francophile jacket with a sequined Eifel Tower on the front and drawings of various other Parisian sights on the back. She was carrying a purple three ring binder.

"Eye on my granddaughter," answered Marti.

"Oh. I'm glad you're both here. As two of my oldest and dearest friends, I want your feedback on some of my ideas," said Siggy. "Now, I've been thinking about my little pies. Do you think I should supply bakeries or freeze them for sales to grocery stores?"

"Hold on Sara Lee...Can we take a few steps back here?" asked Marti.

"Please tell us what your ideal situation would be," asked Caroline.

"Well, since you brought it up, I do like the Sara Lee model. Did you know their products are sold in one hundred and eighty countries? The company has over forty thousand employees worldwide. I think the company was sold in 1957, after seventeen years in business, for nine million dollars. And, Ms. Sara Lee also got over one hundred thousand shares in the new parent company. Not bad, huh?" said Siggy.

Now it was Caroline and Marti's turn to be amazed. Each glanced at the other, and then Caroline spoke first, "So this is what you want?"

"Sure, you work hard, make a great product, and develop a great sales program until some big corporation comes along and buys you out. Then, you have a wonderful retirement income and you get to see the world!" stated Siggy.

"May I ask what's in the binder?" asked Marti.

"It's my business plan. I wanted the two of you to see it before I start looking for investors," answered Siggy, as she handed the binder over to Caroline. "I have some start-up money put away for this, but I figure I'll also need investors."

"Business plan? When did you do this?" asked Marti.

"I've been taking business classes and reading books about small business start-ups for years. I knew that one day I would find *one* recipe that would work. I knew I had to be ready when

I found the right thing. Thanks to all my friends – this time I've got it!

Now, I've got to get to work. I don't want to work at this until I'm eighty, for heaven's sake! I called a realtor friend today to start looking for a good commercial bakery I can rent. I've had suppliers lined up for some time. I just have to get a line of credit to start purchasing and promoting.

What? Why are you two looking at me like that?" Siggy was perplexed by their frozen faces.

"Uh, well...Caroline... you tell her," whispered Marti

"Siggy, I've been away from California for over a decade, and I guess I haven't kept in close enough contact with you; or I just don't remember you telling me that you had been going to classes. I'm absolutely delighted to hear this and well, I am prepared to be your first investor," Caroline said firmly.

"You are? Well that's very sweet of you, dear, but I have such a good feeling about this that I think I'm going for 'Big Money'. I'm going to do this right and fast. But thank you for your vote of confidence," Siggy said buoyantly.

"How much is 'Big Money'?" inquired Caroline.

"Look at page twenty-eight," said Siggy.

Caroline skimmed the rest of the business proposal, found page twenty-eight, cleared her throat, and said "After Robbie reads this proposal and approves it, he will cut a check to get you started. Siggy, we *do* believe in you. Today, Marti and Erik made some calls to see about the Pattie's Pies property. I'd like Robbie to help create a deal on that facility."

"Erik would like to create your logo and run your ad campaign, too. You taught him well, Siggy, and that's not lost on Erik. He has often said his success as a graphic artist came from the encouragement he received from his first art teacher, who he says was you. He will be on board to help you with this new venture," added Marti.

"Caroline, you and Marti are my family. I can't ask you for this kind of money," said Siggy. Tears welled up in her eyes and she leaned toward Marti, and placed her hand over hers.

"Siggy, I haven't said anything about this, but my husband left me a lot of 'Big Money'. Really honey, this is all going to work out for all of us. I just want you to be a great success."

"Am I going to wake up and find myself in the bungalow and this meeting was all just a dream?" whimpered Siggy.

"No baby, you're not. This is all real," promised Marti.

With tears and sighs of relief, the sweet trio of friends embraced each other. Siggy gathered her things and started to leave.

"I'll go with her," said Marti.

"No you won't…we're not finished," said Caroline.

Siggy left the room mumbling to herself all the way down the stairs.

"You need something?" inquired Marti.

"No…now it's time for you," said Caroline.

"Me? Can you pay off the judges so I win the competition, *Miss Big Money*?" chided Marti.

"Marti, of all the women in our group, I have known you the longest. You and I grew up fast and became adults together, and together we've been through highs and lows and the eye of the needle. You are more than a friend; you are another sister to me.

I know why you are delaying your contact with Erik, and I know what you are afraid of," Caroline stated, seriously and lovingly. "I want you to know that I have done something… something that I do not regret."

She placed the file marked 'Siggy' in a drawer and pushed the file marked 'Marti' toward her. She placed her hand on top, to keep it closed. "I am inviting you to go on a trip. We'll work out the dates tomorrow. But for right now, I want you to gather yourself together and be prepared for a telephone call. It will come right here to this phone in a minute. When it does, I want you to take the call. It is Erik…Marti; he is calling you from Sweden. He very much wants to talk with you. I did not tell him about your son. Please Marti, you owe this to yourself, and to your son. I love you very much, and if after my conversation with him this morning, I thought that this in any way would be hurtful to you, I would not have arranged for this call. Pull yourself together,

Marti." Caroline rose from her chair and walked over to Marti. She took a tissue and wiped the tears rolling down Marti's cheeks. She glanced at her watch, and said, "Are you ready?"

Marti nodded. When the phone finally rang, Caroline picked it up and handed it over to Marti. She left the file open for Marti to see – with airline schedules, and a note to purchase tickets to Sweden. Caroline left the room and closed the door behind her.

One True Love

"Let us be grateful to people who make us happy
They are charming gardeners who
Make our souls blossom"

Marcel Proust

*C*aroline walked down to the kitchen and brewed a cup of tea. Her heart was aching for Marti, who was ending a long unbroken silence with the only man she had ever loved. She'd spent her whole adult life keeping her secret, never permitting herself to fall in love with another man. Caroline knew how difficult this was for Marti and how it would be just the beginning of a painful transition to the truth that must follow.

She heard laughter coming from the dining room where Nicole and Paula were meeting with Carmen and JB, and it seemed a comfort. This had been a good day, and tonight would be the last night for this company of friends to have a dinner together, for at least another year. Tomorrow morning, four of the seven would leave AngelFire. After a few moments of solitude, Caroline saw Kate come through the front door.

Kate rounded the kitchen and headed toward the staircase, then caught Caroline in her peripheral vision. "Were we meeting here in the kitchen? I thought your note said to meet you in your office."

"Actually Katie, would you mind walking to the lake again?" asked Caroline.

"I'd love to! I didn't join the others at lunch on the lake today. I met with Robbie. He'll be coming back for dinner tonight, too."

"Good! Would you like some tea, first?" asked Caroline. Kate shook her head 'no', so they quietly left through the back door. "How about riding to the lake on one of our horses?" asked Caroline.

"Sure, that would be great," answered Kate. "I missed whatever horseback riding happened this week. I'm afraid I've not been a very good participant this year."

"Are you kidding?" asked Caroline, without requiring an answer. She led the way to the barn and asked an attendant to have two horses saddled. Kate was a little rusty but still a good rider. In order to extend the ride, this time they took a longer trail to the lake. Caroline noted the vibrancy and the ever present grin on Kate's face. This was a dramatic difference from the Kate who had arrived on Monday in such an exhausted state. Six days of AngelFire, friends, and of course Robbie Collicci, was apparently the perfect prescription for revitalization of the good Doctor Kate. The thought of it all induced a similar grin on Caroline's face.

When they arrived at the lake, they dismounted, and let the horses drink at the shore. Caroline spread a small blanket and invited Kate to sit down next to her.

"Could this day be more beautiful?" asked Kate. "Thank you for hosting this retreat again, Caroline. I so look forward to coming here each year. And this year, WOW! It was just full of surprises! I don't know where to begin." She cleared her throat and said, "I know that Frank's reappearance creates a bittersweet mystery for you, Caroline. Have you figured out what he was trying to tell you? I know Robbie was part of it, but he wouldn't reveal anything. He's very loyal you know."

"He's incredibly loyal," said Caroline. "He's been keeping a safe distance from me for twelve years, in order not to be tempted to reveal any of my husband's secrets. Evidently, Frank has had other sources of income, which he chose not to disclose. Instead, he kept investing that money, and very wisely, with Robbie's help I might add, and together they created quite a legacy.

So today Katie, I have made some investments to help our friends advance toward their dreams. I made all kinds of arrangements and presented some beautiful surprises, but my sweet friend, I am stymied as to what I can do for you. You, I think, are the only person who did not come here facing a crossroads, but may indeed actually be leaving AngelFire standing at onc!

I've never seen you so enamored with a man before. You responded to Robbie the moment you met him. What do you think you are going to do next?"

"I'm going to go home, next. This has been a wonderful week, and I have a lot to think about," answered Kate. "I love my life, Caroline. I gave up on having a partner, a long time ago. My work is meaningful; the clinic is successful, and I love Sonoma. I feel that bringing a man into my life now could make things very complicated."

"Katie, you're not the 'summer fling' type. I've seen you absolutely light up around Robbie. You've laughed and giggled like a school girl all week. Are you going to walk away from the possibility of a serious relationship with him?" asked Caroline.

"I don't know," answered Kate.

"Perhaps you're simply afraid. You have a successful life and maybe you're afraid to change it. You're just afraid of the unknown, honey. We *all are afraid* when it's something new. At this age, we're so set in our ways, we easily resist change. But this is a change for *love*. You're not going to be working at that clinic for the rest of your life, you know." said Caroline.

"I might...there are doctors who work well into their seventies and some do into their eighties," replied Kate.

"Is that your plan? To work until you fall down or just can't do it anymore? Then what? Don't you want to have more time to *enjoy* your life? Have you really thought this through?" implored Caroline. "Robbie Collicci is a good man who adores you. What does *he* want?"

"Uh, well...ultimately, he wants me to come to New Mexico and open a second clinic. He wants us to take a year to be sure about each other, and if we...well, he wants to get married," answered Kate rather sheepishly.

"What? Are you sort of engaged?" asked Caroline.

"Sort of...unofficially, it's too soon to say, and well, we are committed to seeing where this year will take us," whispered Kate.

"Oh my goodness! You must be terrified and no wonder you're panicking! I just lost a husband; Diana's questioning hers; Marti's a mystery case and Siggy well...thank God for Carmen and JB! At least you've seen one solid marriage in front of you this week!" exclaimed Caroline.

"I see lots of solid marriages in my practice, too," said Kate. "Two of my associates are a husband and wife team. I know I'm being resistant now that I have to go back home and face reality. I just need time."

"Time? How many more years do you want to put off knowing real love. Katie, you've never married, never had children. Now you have an opportunity to grow into a new life with someone.

I am walking proof that there are no guarantees for how much time we get to have for anything, or with anyone," pleaded Caroline.

After a moment reflecting on Caroline's words, Kate asked, "Do you think I may have found my one true love?"

"Those are the words of an inexperienced young person, or someone who has read too many romance novels. I'm not sure there is such a thing as a 'one true love' Katie.

I loved Ric Roberts for a long time, and we had children together. We were just not mature enough to know how to handle our problems and at the worst of times, divorce seemed easier. I love my boys, who are now young men, even more than I loved their father. Lots of people say being a grandparent teaches us real love. I loved my work too, Katie. Then I met Frank, and I gave up my career to work with him to build AngelFire. Somehow, I don't think Robbie would ask you to do that," assured Caroline. "Your careers are too different, and he seems so self-sufficient."

"He's is also very careful to reveal little about himself or his past," said Kate.

"Frank was that way, too. I didn't care about his past. I looked at our '*todays and tomorrows*', which seemed much more important to me," confessed Caroline.

"I thought you counted Frank as the love of your life?" asked Kate.

"Frank may have been the love of my millennium," replied Caroline. Her eyes drifted off for a brief moment. *Where did that come from?* she asked herself.

"Katie, you have waited a very long time to even allow yourself to love someone. Tell me how do you feel when you're with Robbie?"

"Well, I feel nervous and relaxed at the same time. No matter what I say, he seems to find it fascinating. We're so different from each other that I'm in a constant state of discovery of another world. I am exceedingly attracted to him; and you're right, it scares me to death! He has lived a very different life than I have," confessed Kate.

"Frank and I had polar opposite worlds, and that didn't mean a thing," said Caroline.

"Robbie really is a wonderful man, and an amazing kisser, I might add... I know I should give this a serious chance. Maybe he would come to Sonoma and see what my life is like," said Kate.

"That may just be the next step," advised Caroline. "Just take it step by step."

"Baby steps, maybe?" joked Kate.

"Katie, look at your life ten or twenty years from now. Would you like to lock up that clinic and go home to your cat and an empty house or would you like to meet your husband for dinner, and then go home together?" asked Caroline.

"That sounds very appealing, and awfully sweet, too," responded Katie. "But it does change a lot of things I had planned."

"Ha! Plans...Schmans! You're talking to the wrong person about plans. All my plans are gone. Actually, you have just given me one possible plan," hinted Caroline.

"What plan is that?" inquired Kate.

"Go ahead, give yourself and Robbie a year to get to know each other, and then decide if you really do love him and want to create a life together. Then let me host the wedding!" she laughed. "I finally know what I can do for you! I promise it will be beautiful! Kate you may have waited your whole life for Robbie Collicci. In the next year, you'll know... S.so, do we have a deal?"

Her hands were shaking, her eyes brimming with tears, but Kate extended her hand and said, "Deal!"

Italian Serenade

"The glory of friendship is not the outstretched hand, nor the kindly smile, nor the joy of companionship; it is the spiritual inspiration that comes to one when you discover that someone else believes in you and is willing to trust you with a friendship." (Adapted)

- Ralph Waldo Emerson

C aroline met with Carmen and JB for a recap of their meeting with *the teacher twins*. They also discussed the menu and entertainment plans for the evening. In delighted anticipation, all three looked forward to the thoughtful, twilight alfresco dinner. They also took a few moments to reflect on the experiences of the week. A week which had produced defining moments for each of them; yet Caroline now knew there was still much more for her to discover.

She retreated to her apartment and drew a long slow, hot bath. She considered pressing the "play" button, but decided to defer to a time when there would be no one to hear the music, no one to know, *if* he appeared again. After an hour of contemplation, she rose out of the warmth of the water, donned a silk gown, slipped into her bed and drifted into a deep and peaceful slumber.

Two hours later, she awoke to the chatter of an excited staff on the AngelFire lawns below her windows. They were setting the stage for the evening's dinner party. They too would enjoy the evening. Caroline chose to stay in the apartment until it was time to appear at the party. She wanted to record the events of the week in her journal. She wondered how far each of her friends would go on their new paths. She, Carmen and JB, would no doubt continue their partnership at AngelFire. Would Diana become a nationally known minister in her own right? Would Siggy be the twenty first century's "*Sara Lee*"? What about Nicole and her new choices? Would the relationship with Paula endure and bring fulfillment? Would Kate actually marry Robbie Collicci? And lastly, Marti, her spiritual sister, could she bring herself to confess to her son the truth about his father? Each arrived at a crossroads in her life. However, did they each choose the right direction? Which of them did not?

For the next hour, Caroline wrote and envisioned possibilities for her friends, but was not able to imagine what was next in her own future.

Then her heart and thoughts turned to Frank. What did she mean when she told Katie "*he was the love of her millennium?*" Caroline continued writing, recording her thoughts about Frank.

Frank and I had something different from the very first time we met. I was incredibly attracted to him. We had something deeper than anything I had ever experienced, something sacred.

We didn't have to cultivate it or develop it. We honored it. It was already there, as if we had known each other a thousand years. It included passion but went beyond passion.

I don't even know if there are words to describe the depth of our togetherness. We were intrinsically woven together. It was like there was this 'eternal us', this 'naturalness' and we had been given another opportunity to experience it. Does this make any sense?

Perhaps this is why I feel hollow now, as though organs are missing from my body.

I don't think this comes along in life very often. Maybe it was a maturation of love – with a wordless understanding.

Caroline took a moment to regain her composure as she realized she had stopped writing, had been drifting off in the memories of their life together. She wrote one last note to herself.

Yes, Frank may have been the love of my millennium, which assures me we will meet again.

This I know to be true. Sometime, some place...we will meet again.

Caroline set aside her journal to prepare for the joyful evening ahead, in the company of loving friends. But before doing so, she made one more telephone call. "Julia, it's Caroline, I'm coming to California next week, and I want to come to Santa Barbara and talk to you. Yes, I have a great deal of good news to share with you. Listen, I don't think I will be able to make it for the Alaskan cruise...I know...but I may be going to Europe. Can you clear your calendar for about a month and live out a dream with me? Yes, In January...we'll leave from Ft. Lauderdale, Florida. Do you think you can stand a full thirty days with me? Bring David? Of course. Okay...we'll talk when I get there... And Julia...I love you."

Under the direction of Carmen and JB, the staff had created an enchanting setting for the dinner. Italian patio lights had been strung across two immense cottonwood trees, and a large dining table heavily draped in white linens had been placed between them. Traditional New Mexico *luminarias* defined the perimeter of the space. A collection of large and small votive candles on the table would soon be lit to complete this luminous landscape. A wrought iron planter, filled with ice, chilled the wines for the evening. Eleven place settings awaited their guests. The stemware glistened as the sun began to set. Water goblets were laced with iced lemon and lime slices. Before long, the moonlight would appear and complete the perfect ambience of the evening.

Caroline came downstairs in a long black halter dress, adorned with a grand vintage silver and turquoise Zuni squash blossom necklace, which had been a gift from Carmen and JB. They met her with smiles and full hearts, in the lobby of the AngelFire Inn. Their somber silence conveyed the unspoken emotions each of them felt. Carmen's ensemble was another stunning, embroidered and beaded traditional Zuni dress. JB had donned a suede jacket with similar embroidery.

They heard distant voices and a classical guitarist, who began to play his lilting Latin music. Together, they walked toward the grand AngelFire lawns to host the final dinner of this year's retreat. Eight smiling faces were waiting.

Diana and Jackson were the first to greet them. Diana, without surprise, was strikingly beautiful in a vivid coral, long-sleeved, knit evening dress. The ballet neckline revealed a startling single diamond pendant held by a wide gold chain. Jackson chose to be more casual, as his daily attire included a suit and tie. His beautifully tailored and monogrammed white shirt needed nothing more. He amiably embraced Caroline and asked about her sons.

"Robbie and I are going to California to see them on Monday," she responded. "I've only told them I had something very important to share with them. They will be astonished when Robbie and I give them the news. Thank you Jackson, for asking about my boys."

Jackson escorted the three lovely ladies toward the dinner setting, while JB consulted with the staff. Caroline was stopped by the incandescent smiling Siggy. She wore a boldly printed caftan in summer colors of lime, yellow and orange. Caroline had never seen her happier. Siggy was sure to be the center of joy and laughter for the evening.

Nicole and Paula strolled arm and arm onto dining area but broke quickly to mingle with the others. They were the *pajaros azul* of the night. Harmonized shades of cobalt and amethyst were intricately woven into their patterned and fringed jackets. Though the jackets were styled quite differently, they were constructed from the same fabric.

Caroline acquired her first glass of wine and searched for Marti. To her great pleasure, she found Marti out of her traditional black attire, and wearing a tea length, pink, slit sleeve tunic and skirt. She had added beads to her braids and wore pink and white bracelets. Their sustained embrace and the look in Marti's eyes told Caroline the call had accomplished something wonderful. They said nothing, as they wanted no tears on this night.

The staff asked everyone to be seated, and the wine was poured around the table.

Caroline sat at the head of the table, and JB sat at the other end, where Frank would have been. She rose to speak, "As our traditions continue, tonight we will enjoy a *Bella Italian* dinner in honor of my husband Frank. He always loved this night... not because you were all leaving," she said wryly. "But because he loved to show off his own culinary talents. Frank has been an unexpected guest this week, and a benefactor to all of us. So, while I'd like to propose a toast to tonight's Italian Chef, Roberto Niccolini, I would also propose a toast to Frank Amoroso. Where ever you are, we are in gratitude for your wisdom, your love and your generosity." Glasses clinked and cheers and smiles dismissed any solemnity for the moment. Then Caroline spoke again, "Reverend Greene would you like to give a blessing this evening?"

Jackson began to stand, but was halted. "I think she means me," whispered Diana.

"Oh, of course," he graciously replied. Diana thanked him, rose and said heartfelt words of gratitude and praise for Angel-Fire and its hosts. She added appreciative words for the shared moments of grace between each of those at the table. She asked for safe journeys as they returned to their homes. She affirmed blessings for futures filled with joy and beauty. In that moment, Diana was spiritual elegance manifested.

The music resumed, and members of the staff were the first to speak as they served warm crusty bread with olive oil and tapenades. Calamari arrived next, with chopped celery, olive oil, wine and lemon. Cups of marinara sauce were added for dipping. Ravioli Burro e Salvia filled with spinach and ricotta cheese and drizzled with a sage butter, followed. Gasps of pure delight sent clear messages back to *la cucina and Chef Niccolini.* The staff outdid themselves with fine service, and since they were welcome to converse with the guests, they brought additional humor and interest to the conversation.

For a more regional dish, locally caught trout was poached in white wine, and served with lemon and capers. The entrées were accompanied by side dishes of small salads and a shrimp stew over black squid linguini.

Caroline glanced at Carmen each time a course was served; both took pleasure in knowing they had found Frank's culinary replacement in Chef Niccolini.

As the plates were cleared, before the desert was presented, JB rose to speak. "First, I would like to acknowledge Ricardo Estevez, our guitarist who has played so beautifully. I'd also like to thank our staff for their excellent service, and ask that they send for our wonderful chef.

This is the twelfth year for this gathering of these fine women, and I must say each year is different. I never know what to expect! What I've come to understand about these women, is that each of you works hard at what you love, and love the life you live. It is the same for Carmen and me. We love AngelFire, and we're always glad when you're here."

Carmen followed her husband's sentiments and said, "Each year when you come to AngelFire, we follow tradition. There are many things that we do every year, although I doubt that this year could ever be repeated. This year, when we looked for the best entertainment for the farewell dinner, we chose time-honored classical traditions. This weekend is the beginning of the Angel-Fire Summer Music Festival, and so tonight on behalf of Caroline, JB and me, we present you with tickets to a special concert. After the desert, we will bring the van out to the front of the Inn, and we will drive over to the concert hall." Everyone was thrilled with the idea.

Caroline rose to speak next, "I see our chef has arrived. Roberto, please say hello to our guests." Roberto Niccolini was a soft spoken man, who gently bowed his head, shook hands and thanked Caroline, Carmen and JB. The staff refilled the wine glasses one last time, and began to serve the dessert, which was Panna Cotta with fresh berries.

Caroline remained standing, lifted her glass for a toast, and said, "When I was a little girl in the girl scouts, we used to sing a song about friends which referred to new friends as silver and old friends as "gold". Being too young to have 'old friends', we probably didn't give much thought to what this meant, but it definitely planted the seeds for the value of good friends.

Gold has been the treasure of the ages, and you, my friends, are the '*gold*' in my life. You have guided, nurtured and influenced my life just by being who you are. I love the best in you; you love the best in me, and I stand in absolute gratitude for your presence in my life. You are part of all that I find sacred and true. My toast to you is my hope for you, that each of you is always able to be all of who you are, and all you are meant to be."

In another expression of gratitude, Siggy sspoke, "I want to say something. I know that most years, I've been kind of the comic relief of this group, but you're all like family to me. I know I was there for you Caroline, when your children were little, and Marti and Erik have always been a regular part of my family. I love that our friendships have continued long past diapers and runny noses; ...our kids, that is. And Nicole, I've known you since you were a teenager and you've become a fine intelligent woman. Diana, I want to thank you for all the hopeful letters you have written me over the years since I started to include you as one my taste testers. No one gave me better reviews or more encouraging words. Now, finally with the help of my friends, I am going into business. I want you all to know that I am really ready for this. I am prepared, and I am willing to be the successful baker I believe I am meant to be. From now on you will no longer be receiving experimental recipes. Instead, you'll be getting my newsletter from my website with a message from Sigrid Kerrington at www.sigridsweets.com."

The table of friends roared with cheers for her success.

Nicole and Paula rose together, of course, and of course, Nicole spoke first. "As you know, we're not leaving tomorrow and have decided to begin a new life and possibly new careers here in New Mexico. Next year, we'll no doubt have an exciting report to share on our progress." She turned to Paula, whose voice was already beginning to crack as she spoke, "I don't know where or when in my life I have felt this kind of acceptance. I'm embarrassed to confess that I came here with much resistance, and now it looks like I may have the possibility of a dream come true, which I too, hope to share with you next year." She couldn't talk any further, so Nicole put her arm around her and they both sat down.

Diana and Jackson also rose together and Jackson lifted his glass, "I want to toast to Caroline, who opened my eyes to something I could not see. Diana and I will leave AngelFire in the morning, to go home and pack, for we are planning to go away to spend some important TIME together. We will remember who we are, and we will never forget you." Diana raised her glass and simply said, "Thank you Caroline...for *everything*."

Katie sprang from her seat to say, "This week has been as delicious as this wonderful dinner tonight. I came here this year expecting to rest, have some good food, and all the usual laughter we share together. Did I say *Rest?* Did *anybody* get any rest this week?

During our rock band night, Siggy and I sang the song '*When Will I Be Loved*?' We tried to sound like Linda Ronstadt, but

I think we sounded more like the Muppets go to Nashville. I hope the Everly Brothers will forgive us. Well, my questions got answered this week. I am loved, by all of you and my new love, Robbie." She looked at him adoringly and said "I have no idea where this is going, but as a result of meeting you, I feel wonderful! So thank you Caroline, Carmen and JB. This was the best year yet!"

"Watch out Katie, it may just get even *better,*" warned Carmen laughingly.

Marti was the last to speak; she rose, flipped her braids, searched for her words and said, "I uh…couldn't be happier, for all of you. Really, I…I know there were things that happened this week that changed your lives. Something happened for me this week, too. But it didn't change my life; it stopped it." For a brief moment all were silent. "I created a life for myself, with Caroline by my side, many…too many, years ago. I left all I knew behind and created an illusion that my son has lived with his entire life. Today, it stopped. The door to the truth has been opened. In a few weeks, I will take the next step to restart my life. I will travel to Sweden and I… I…" Caroline and Katie wrapped their arms around Marti and said, "There's no need to say anymore."

Carmen quickly stood and said, "Okay everyone, we still have a concert to go to!" She handed her guests envelopes with her hand written invitations and festival tickets. "JB has gone to get the van," she said, trying to hurry the crowd toward the front of the Inn.

Marti composed herself, while Siggy blotted her eyes carefully, to keep her mascara from running down her face this time. Robbie wrapped his jacket around Kate's shoulders and led her toward the van. The excitement of the evening resumed as they boarded the van.

Diana was the first to open the envelope. It read:

You are cordially invited to the AngelFire Music Festival
Enclosed are your tickets for tonight's concert…

Saturday, August 22
United Church of AngelFire, AngelFire, New Mexico
MUSICAL CONVERSATIONS I
Mountain Serenades I
BARBER
Serenade for Strings, Op. 1
Music from AngelFire Strings
BEETHOVEN
Serenade in D Major for Flute, Violin and Viola, Op. 25
Tara Helen O'Connor, Flute; Ani Kavafian, Violin; Paul Neubauer, Viola
HUGO WOLF
Italian Serenade for Strings *Music from AngelFire Strings*

With Love,
Caroline, Carmen & JB

Nicole read the program and asked, "Caroline, did you arrange for the Italian music tonight, too?"

"What?" started Caroline. She read the program for the first time and smiled. She turned and looked over to Robbie and winked. "No, I didn't actually, but Frank may have had something to do with it." Robbie smiled in return.

The music hall was just a short drive from the Inn. The performance was sold out, and the troupe of eleven had to sit near the back of the hall. Caroline sat on the end of the row, next to Carmen. The two of them nodded 'hellos' and waves to fellow AngelFire proprietors. Caroline pointed to the listing of the Italian Serenade, leaned over to Carmen and whispered, "He probably requested this from the AngelFire Strings at last year's music festival. It wasn't just Patsy Cline he liked." Carmen nodded in agreement. Just before the music began, Caroline squeezed Carmen's hand and said softly, "Another wonderful evening, Carmen, beautifully done."

The audience hushed, the room darkened and the violinists began to play. Caroline's mind drifted back to previous AngelFire Music Festivals and the pride they brought to the small mountain community. She cast her eyes to the left and watched her friends engrossed in the beauty of the music. Paula's right hand was lifted slightly and waving with the music as if she were conducting from her chair. Marti sat next to her fellow musician exchanging whispers. Siggy sat smiling, enjoying the music and was no doubt wondering if her sweets would be served at next year's festival. Robbie and Katie sat hand in hand, and Jackson and Diana exchanged a smile.

It has been a very good week; And Peace and Peace and Peace, be everywhere...she thought.

As the Italian Serenade began, Caroline felt a blush of warmth on her cheek. It was what usually happened just before she sensed Frank's presence. Perhaps it was a kiss...

About thirty feet away,
stood a specter of light in the outline of a man.
He remained still, undetectable.
No one could see him.
No one ever would.
As he watched her,
enfolding her in his love,
he vowed he would watch over her
keep her safe
and never break her heart again.

JB, stirred in his seat, taking Carmen's hand
and said, "Everything is going to be all right"
Caroline overheard him and smiled.
"Yes, I know that now," she said.

Forthcoming in Book II

"The splendor of friendship comes in the realization that someone else believes in you —

And your dreams"

*T*he women of AngelFire have gracefully dealt with grief, loss, and family heartbreak. Each of the company of friends must act upon their golden opportunities and recreate their destiny. None feels the invincibility of youth, but the exquisite connectedness and empowerment of their camaraderie, sustained by the Divine.

In the pages of The Women of AngelFire – Book Two, the women will delve deeper and risk all they know, to move onward toward meaningful, purposeful changes for that "*Dream-come-true*" state. Yet, sometimes our dreams come true and create unanticipated circumstances that make us question everything.

Within the next year of their lives, they will recognize and deal with issues regarding the challenges of success, the acceptance of age, beauty and even a little plastic surgery!

Revelations of one's worthiness surface as new levels of prosperity evokes past beliefs, especially for JB and Carmen.

Caroline, still in her season of grief, now has her grand fortune to govern, and the mystery that intertwines both.

Siggy redefines herself completely and is a joy to write.

Marti's challenges come as truths are revealed for both Erik Jr. and Sr.

Nicole and Paula, inner directed and service minded, experience an inexplicable interruption.

And for the first time in her life, Kate must decide on a commitment to love, of another kind.

Ah yes...there will be more laughter, beauty and music, and the expressions of Mother Nature herself.

Book Club Topics & Queries

Scene 1 – Caroline & Frank..........
In the process of grief, a person often yearns for the return of a lost loved one. Some may feel the presence of that person in unexpected ways. Is this real? Is it the dreamer within? Can love pull back the spirit of a loved one?

Scene 2 – Carmen & Julia.......
Caroline's sister Julia is quirky, sincere and protective. Is she a rare bird in today's world? Carmen is a 'rock' and everyone should have "a Carmen" in her life. Who is your Carmen? Or are you someone's Carmen?

Scene 3 – Marti .....
If you remember the 60's & 70's, you will remember the disgrace of the out of wedlock pregnancy, not to mention the stigma of interracial couples. Marti's parents reacted as many did during that period. Book I in the series, does not acknowledge the sacrifice Caroline made for Marti by moving to California. What do you think that was like for Caroline during that era? What do you think about Marti's keeping the truth about Erik's father a secret?

Scene 4 – Sigrid....
Siggy is the consummate resourceful single mom. Through her creativity, she transformed her grief over her husband betrayal and the divorce that followed. She enters numerous contests and constantly created projects for herself and the children she cared for. What a prosperity lesson! She believed in herself and didn't give up! Have you ever had to create a new life for yourself? Did you discover new excitement through your own creativity?

Scene 5 – Diana.....
Diana represents beauty and grace. She holds her behavior to extremely high standards; yet, in the face of her husband's possible infidelity, she is as vulnerable as the rest of us. Do you think she overreacted? Capitulated? There's much more to this story in Book II!

Scene 6 – Dinner for Five, Six or Seven....
This was a "let your hair down" night for this circle of friends, revealing each woman's personal crisis. Out of this chapter came the author's quote "The salve that soothes a broken heart is often the company of a good friend." Friends can provide a safety net when we're feeling most vulnerable. It requires loyalty and trust without judgment. Are you that "safety net" for someone? Perhaps you would like to acknowledge the person who may have been a "safety net" for you.

Scene 7 – Last Confession....
The stoic JB has passed judgment on these women and created his own Zuni cure...thank God for sopapillas and honey! Kate's immediate response to Robbie Collicci was as much of a surprise to her as it was to her friends. Why do some of us have that "Love at first sight" experience? Is it fantasy? Real? Or miracle?

Scene 8 – Now what...
This group of women has further relaxed their inhibitions and become a female rock band! Did you find the idea entertaining?

Did you know the lyrics and melodies? Would you ever dream of doing the same with your friends?

Scene 9 – JB....
JB's spiritual nature has left him open to sense Frank's presence. His guilt for not saving Frank seems unreasonable; yet, in the grieving process, don't we all internalize that "woulda-coulda-shoulda" dialogue? Some men say they can compartmentalize their grief? Is that your experience?

Scene 10 – Nicole...
Nicole lives fiercely, standing up for everything she believes in and there is purpose in all she does. She is an admirer of women like Betty Friedan, Gloria Steinem, and Rosa Parks, but her brilliance in math and science leads her to inspire young women for careers in those fields. Nicole's willingness to enter a relationship with another woman is easily accepted by her friends, but not quite understood by Caroline. Would you have been willing to have that conversation, as Caroline did with Nicole?

Scene 11 – Possibilities...
Kate tells Diana..."The first step in getting what you want, is knowing what you want" Why is it that sometimes it is so hard for us to figure that out? Can we make those decisions without feeling selfish?

Scene 12 – Peak Experience...
Heeeeres Frank!....He just can't seem to move on yet....kind of makes you think twice about taking your secrets to the grave... doesn't it?

Scene 13 – Kate & Robbie...
Kate wants an evening of getting to know Robbie better...she anticipates further romantic possibilities....Then we read about "the kiss". What is it about that kiss that moves this relationship

forward? Is it the way he kisses her? Or her willing surrender? Hhmmmm...

Scene 14 – On to the Summit....
This scene was about being still and going within one's self to find the answers needed to move forward. Where do you go for that mountain top experience when you are at a crossroads?

Scene 15 – New Beginnings and The End...
Each of the women reveals decisions they made while up on the mountain. Were there any surprises? Then, a thunderstorm that culminates in the merging of Frank and Caroline--one last time. Isn't that what two lovers want at the end of life? One last time?"

Scene 16 – Revelations...
Caroline pulls up her bootstraps, confronts the truth, and discovers that she is the heir to a grand fortune. Although her head is spinning with questions, she is still able to make some quick decisions. What would you do if this kind of information was revealed to you? Would it change your feelings about your lost loved one?

Scene 17 – Sorting What's Real...
The company of friends has witnessed what may be termed an authentic paranormal experience and agrees to keep the story to themselves. Wouldn't you want to tell someone?

Scene 18 – Revelation Revealed...
Caroline's generosity is in full throttle! She begins by rewarding Carmen and JB, who are genuinely grateful and equally astonished. At this point there must be many questions running through their minds about Frank ...Ya'think?

Scene 19 – Dinner at Eight for Eleven...
Exhausted, confused, and even bewildered, Caroline, Carmen and JB host a dinner at the country club. Caroline and friends

announce their endorsement of Sigrid's final attempt at a sweet treat. Note: The author bought the pans and attempted to make these little treats and it was a lot of work!

Scene 20 – The Determined Launch...
Caroline formulates her plans...enlists Marti's help... and through her generosity transforms her sorrow through the joy of giving. This book is about transformation; Caroline demonstrates a great example...What is the first thing you would do if you inherited millions of dollars?

Scene 21 – Notes to My Friends
Caroline sends heartfelt notes to her friends, which includes an invitation to meet with her as she offers each of them a Golden Opportunity. If you wrote a similar note to a friend, what would it say? What Golden Opportunity would you offer to your closest friend?

Scene 22 – Time
In an attempt to side rail a potential disaster in the Greene's marriage, Caroline offers them the gift of focused TIME together. Was she too pushy or was this an act of desperation stemming from her own grief? Would you agree that all marriages could use regular R & R and recommitment?

Scene 23 – Choices
How many great ideas do not come to fruition due to the lack of funds? Caroline's offer to be Nicole's Angel Investor, became an opportunity to give back to her sister-in-law. The fruition of Paula's Golden Opportunity was essentially up to her own performance, (and it never hurts to have connections!). Have you ever been given what you needed to start a project by someone who believes in you? Would you invest in a friend's idea?

Scene 24 – Sweet Trio
The Golden Opportunities continue with Siggy's Symphony Sweets...Were you surprised at how prepared she was? Isn't this

what we are supposed to do when we have a dream? Gather as much information as possible; explore your options; put all elements in place... and prepare for the realization of a dream...It could happen to you!

Marti was given an opportunity to tell the truth......Does she have the courage to go through with it?

Scene 25 – One True Love
It looks like Kate has been swept off her feet! Even in this decade, women still use the term "The One", when they have fallen in love. Do you believe that there is a real aspect of "knowing," when choosing a life partner? Or are we still following a myth?

Scene 26 – Italian Serenade
One last grand finale dinner and concert; one last time for Frank and Caroline. Each of the women has made possible life-changing decisions. Each is acknowledged and comforted by the support of her friends. These are women of faith, of courage, and of grace. Which of them has the odds against her? Who will triumph? Why?

*The Women of AngelFire, Book
Two – answers all those questions!*

The glory of friendship is not the outstretched hand, nor the kindly smile, nor the joy of companionship; it is the spiritual inspiration that comes to one when you discover that someone else believes in you and is willing to trust you with a friendship. (Adapted)
- Ralph Waldo Emerson

Made in the USA
Charleston, SC
03 June 2013